JERI SHEPHERD

COOPER RIDGE

THE WONDER KID

This is a work of fiction. Names, characters, places, and incidents either are the product of the author's imagination or are used fictitiously. Any resemblance to actual persons, living or dead, events, or locales is entirely coincidental.

First edition of book released in 2008. Editorial and visual updates have been implemented for this second edition.

Copyright © 2008, 2023 by Regina Laberge

All rights reserved. In accordance with the U.S. Copyright Act of 1976, no part of this book may be reproduced in any form on by an electronic or mechanical means, including information storage and retrieval systems, without permission in writing from the copyright owner, except by a reviewer who may quote brief passages in a review.

If you would like to use passages of the book for purposes other than review, please direct requests to JeriShepherdBooks@gmail.com with the subject line: RIGHTS – COOPER RIDGE. We thank you for supporting the rights of this author and of all artists and creatives and just be cool, man.

Cover Design by: Enchanted Quill Press
ISBN 13: 979-8985696035

From Jeri Shepherd Books –
A Lucy's Lantern Literature Imprint
www.redwritesbooks.com.com

Author and publisher are not responsible for content on websites or social media platforms that are not owned by the author or publisher.

Printed in the U.S.A.

To the victims of the Waukesha Christmas Parade tragedy. The wonder and inspiration of your recoveries is a dream worthy of the fireflies. Let us send many such joys to the heavens for the six angels no longer with us.   #waukeshastrong

Cooper Ridge, The Wonder Kid

REJI LABERJE

Cooper Ridge, The Wonder Kid originally released in 2008 under my pen name, REJI LABERJE. When I relaunched my solo author career after a stint of a dozen years in nonfiction and biography writing alongside many incredible men and women, I looked at the titles worthy of a facelift. The resurrection of *Cooper Ridge* was at the top of my list. I was proud to revisit this fantasy originally inspired by the Mysteries of Harris Burdick illustration *"Archie Smith, Boy Wonder"* from the book by Chris Van Allsburg.

This book doesn't just come to you with a new cover. More characters, more content, and some interesting changes have taken this book that was already popular and given it new life for a new audience. Even if you were a fan of the original, there will be something for you to love in this second edition.

Thank you for reading and keep on doing it! I appreciate every one of my readers.

– Five Stars –

* * * * *

"I love dreams, their power to transport and transform, and you'll be hard-pressed to not think about this story at least a little the next time you close your eyes"

– Dennis Vogen, Author, Artist, & Publisher

https://www.jerishepherdbooks.com/books

One Author
Two Names
Many Titles

To Cooper, his dreams of an ordinary
life were some of his most
peaceful and satisfying imaginings.

Chapter 1

Cooper Ridge, The Wonder Kid

Cooper was having the game of his life. By the third inning, he had caught three flies that came his way out there in deep left field. He had assisted on two double plays by the bottom of the fourth, and—in the top of the fifth—he batted in the run that put his team, The Washington Wonder-boys, up by one.

Victory hung like a cold glass of lemonade out of reach in the perfect seventy-degree air that flowed in gentle breezes, carrying the scent of hot dogs and popcorn, over the little league field. They wanted it. They could see it, feel it, taste it . . . but not reach it . . . not yet.

The sun shone warmly down on the back of the young Wonderboy's neck. Cooper's dad, burnt from the weeks spent watching his son play ball, paced back and forth in front of the silver, metal, bench-style bleachers. They were full to capacity and lined up as deep as a stadium behind the chain link fence that separated the spectators from the little league pride of western Washington state. Everybody in the community had come out to show their support.

Cooper's best friend, Matt Hill, spun the ball in his chalked up left hand. That lefty had also had a great game. In the past though, Matt had choked when the win was this close. Cooper tried to send positive thoughts his friend's way across the dust-stirred grass field. The tension was so thick that he could nearly feel the energy bounce right off the diamond and back to him. Matt shuffled his feet on the mound, shifting his weight from right to left and back again. It was a sign of exhaustion and anxiety Cooper had often noticed in his friend. The other team, on Matt's last pitch to the previous batter, had stolen a base and now the tying run was on third with the win on first. The count was full for this batter; three balls, two strikes. If Matt could get off just one more strike, the Wonderboys would remain champs for one more year of glory. They would be treated as kings rather than the young men they were.

At last, Matt took a heavy breath, deeply shrugged his shoulders, and lowered his eyes, tightening his focus on the home plate. Cooper sensed the conviction rising above the anxiety. Matt had played the full little league regulation six innings.

Cooper braced his knees; he was at the ready in a half-squat with his arms loose. He swallowed hard. His saliva was thin, warm, and salty and the gulp only added to the butterflies in his stomach. He knew that Matt's fastball was the best in the league, but Cooper felt like an eternity passed in that moment after the pitch left his friend's hand. He prepared himself to push off into a run as heard the crack of the bat against the ball echo in his ears.

Time stood still.

He was sure the crowd must be roaring, but in his world, Cooper's only focus was on the ball coming toward him. He imagined hearing the whir of it buzzing through the air. The space around the white sphere became blurry and the ball itself seemed to grow larger as it neared.

It was over Matt, past the shortstop and not anywhere near foul or center. It was Cooper's play, no doubt. He couldn't move deep enough, left enough, fast enough toward the now falling baseball. He could nearly see the stitches. He felt every muscle quiver as he raced to the would-be homer, and simultaneously spotted the runner on third making his way to a homerun.

That opponent seemed to be moving more quickly toward his goal than Cooper was to his own. In fact, he felt certain he was moving in slow motion. As the stiches on that fly came into focus and it began to lose its wings though, Cooper gained his. With an amazing push for a kid of sixteen, he was airborne. Cooper stretched his tall body and extended his long arm to its maximum reach.

With a resounding SMACK, a beautiful sting ran from his palm down his arm, to his shoulder, down his spine, and through his legs straight into his tingling toes that then slammed into the ground followed by the rest of his collapsing body.

He had the ball.

As he clumsily stood up in disbelief, the rest of Cooper's world beyond the ball came back into focus. The cheering and applause of the crowd was deafening. He wasn't sure if it had just begun or if it had been going all along. Cooper leapt high in the air, oblivious to any game pains, to loud background chants of "WONDER KID! WONDER KID!"

It was a title he had earned this season and he was proud to hear it called while his teammates rushed him.

"WONDER KID! WONDER KID!"

Cooper heard the cry over the cheers and hoots of his fellow players and over the roaring crowd outside the fence. He was sure his dad was out there hugging some stranger or other, squeezing the air out of them while he pointed out his son.

Matt and the other boys jumped and screamed when their coaches joined the huddle.

"WONDER KID! WONDER KID!" the chant continued.

Finally, pushing between the broad shoulders of the ball players, Cooper spotted his proud father grinning uncontrollably. Instead of the half hugs that are acceptable for fathers and sons, anything goes after a winning competition. Cooper's dad pulled him down off a set of shoulders upon which he'd been hoisted, and he pulled him into a full bear hug. The man held his son back and looked into the crystal blue eyes nestled deep in his tanned face. As such an athletic boy, Cooper was already the spitting image of his young dad. The leftfielder smiled back.

"WONDER KID! WONDER KID!" the calls boomed around the Ridge men.

The elder Ridge pushed Cooper's hat backward off his head and he ruffled his son's thick, brown mop top.

"WONDER KID! WONDER KID!"

The Wonderboys team members continued cheering even as the exiting crowds began to quiet. Mr. Ridge placed a flat, hard kiss on his son's forehead and Cooper didn't even mind that it was in front of the team.

"I am so proud! That's my boy they're all cheering! The Wonder Kid! My son, Danny Mills. Danny Mills, The Wonder Kid," he gleamed.

Cooper cocked his head in confusion. His father's face began to fade, followed by the little league scene that surrounded him. He turned his head shame-fully to one said and—just before feeling that familiar, warm tickle in his ear, the distant, muffled echoes continued: "DANNY MILLS, THE WONDER KID! DANNY MILLS, THE WONDER KID . . . ."

Chapter 2

Elation To Bitterness

Cooper opened his eyes in a state of disorientation, and he shook his head back and forth. It was the only part of his body that he could move since a car accident eight years ago. He was paralyzed from the neck down. The same accident had killed his father. From the time he was eight, Cooper felt like little more than a very wild imagination attached to a very idle body.

Of course, that's not how those in his life treated him. He knew better, but he couldn't help his mind from going there after his dreams. The dreams felt so alive that, when he awoke from them, he couldn't help but feel like part of him had died all over again. It was like he was waking from the coma all over again. Unable to move for the first time all over again.

Tonight, in his dream, Cooper got to be one of his very favorite characters, The Wonder Kid.

Sometimes, in his dreams, Coop was a regular student in a regular school with regular friends. Sometimes, he ran and played frisbee with the dog that lived down the block, and sometimes—on quiet nights—he would simply dream he was taking a walk down a cool calm street in town, maybe with Ashley by his side, holding his hand. Just a simple walk. Simple to anyone who could do it anyway. To Cooper, his dreams of an ordinary life were some of his most peaceful and satisfying imaginings.

Tonight though, he didn't dream about being ordinary. He dreamed he was extraordinary. When Cooper was The Wonder Kid, he was a hero. He swore down to the soles of his feet that he really felt his arms moving; he really felt his legs pounding the ground; he really felt his heart throbbing in his chest. Most of all, during those dreams, he really felt . . . joy.

Then the dream would end, and the nightmare would begin – the nightmare that was his life. Somebody in his dream would call him by the name Danny Mills. Then, he would be snapped back to the reality that he was not Cooper Ridge, The Wonder Kid. In fact, he was not even Cooper Ridge the student or Cooper Ridge who played with the neighborhood dog. He was not even the ordinary boy walking down an ordinary street on an ordinary night in town. He felt like Cooper Ridge, The Worthless Kid.

When he awoke from those hero dreams, always after a warm tickle in the ear that was not against his pillow, his elation would immediately melt away to bitterness.

Cooper heard a tiny motor and a rushing of air. It was his mattress. It was programmed to fill and release air to and from different chambers within it every fifteen minutes. This made sure that his body didn't get bedsores from the constant pressure of his own weight lying against the mattress. The bedsores, or pressure sores, would need to be drained of the blister-like juices or they could lead to serious infections or even the need to cut away his own tissue.

As the sound of the flowing air ceased, he realized that the tickle in his ear itched and needed to be scratched. Cooper turned his head and pushed the offending ear hard against his pillow. Then he nodded to scratch, much as a bear would rub against a tree trunk to soothe a back itch. Cooper huffed a self-pitying sigh as the thought that a bear had more value in life than he did passed through his mind. If he shared those kinds of thoughts with his family, he'd end up back in sessions with the psychologist. He didn't mind the appointments and even liked the doctor, but the idea of one more thing in his schedule was overwhelming.

It's not that Cooper was a negative person. And he certainly wasn't being fed low self-worth beliefs by those in his life. He lived a pretty good life. The depression usually only made its voice heard in his own head. He couldn't stop it there.

He arched his neck and rolled back his eyes to read the glowing green numbers on the clock over his bed. It was 4:30 in the morning. His mother wouldn't be up for another hour and a half. He put his head back down. There was no point in pretending that he could do more than lay there.

He didn't know whether he was angrier at himself for having the dream or jealous of Danny Mills for being the "real" Wonder Kid. As he lay there staring at the ceiling, he wished that tonight's dream had only been about Cooper Ridge, Ordinary Kid.

Chapter 3

The Morning Routine

He may have dozed back to sleep. Cooper wasn't sure. If he did, it was a dreamless sleep and that was a good thing.

At 6:oo, Cooper began hearing the familiar sounds of the morning routine. First, there was the annoying beep of his mother's alarm, then her shuffling hand on the nightstand, followed by her fumbling slap on the snooze button. It would be seven minutes of quiet before the beginning of the other signs of the start of a new day.

Cooper was good at listening, and at watching. Before he could move his chair on his own and when he would be at family gatherings, he'd often say how unoffended he was to be left in one room when everybody else went to another. Then, alone, all he'd have to do is listen and watch. He rarely called for them, those who left him behind. He found it embarrassing, like a baby crying to be taken from his crib. Eventually, somebody would say something, and they'd realize Cooper had been left. His mother usually would return, apologizing for thinking a cousin had been with him.

Cooper never got upset about being left alone when he had good conversations to observe . . . good views to take in. He didn't like it much when he was left in a bland room with no sound or sights to distract him from his loneliness, but that was not usually the case. He found that, if he really focused his mind, he could find something with which to be creative and thoughtful.

Coop assumed he had a greater appreciation for all of his senses because he didn't have the ability to use his arms and legs. Oh, it wasn't always that way. When he'd first gotten injured and then, months later, when he realized he was permanently disabled, he could only long for and focus on the lacks that he had in his ability, rather than on the gains. But eventually, he found new ways to interact with his world. There were days when he'd get taken for a walk in the park and he'd catch himself completely enraptured in another person's moment, listening to and watching the person.

Cooper rolled his head and eyes back again to read the clock. He sighed. It was 6:14 when he heard his mother's slippered feet sweeping down the hardwood floors of the hallway. Hardwood. That was a necessity. He couldn't stand carpeted homes. They rarely worked well with his chair. This morning, his mother must have needed an extra snooze. Cooper's mom creaked his door open slowly and tiptoed across the room to his window where she opened the baseball-motif curtains and pulled up the shade to reveal the open window (which was how Cooper liked it to be left while he slept and, living in Arizona, this wasn't a problem for most of the year).

The morning light shone on the walls that were also covered with baseball pennants from all of Cooper's favorite World Series winning teams. He wasn't a fan loyal to a single team. He didn't have specific-colored jerseys or logos. He liked the game. He liked watching the players that made a difference out on the field. He enjoyed the athleticism and the magic that took place in a particularly exciting game regardless of who was on the field.

His mother looked at her pride and joy. "Hey Bud," she whispered with a smile. "You're already awake. I hope it hasn't been long," she added as she sat next to her son on the bed.

"No," he lied. Cooper hated the sound of his voice in the morning before he sat up. He was always hoarse, and the words gargled out with an unattractive blend of phlegm. He slept propped up a little bit on pillows, but it wasn't enough. "I heard your alarm is all."

"You look good this morning," his mom's voice was sweet. "I swear the color in your cheeks is wonderful. You sneaking off to play ball games at night or something?" she joked.

Cooper's mind flashed back to one of his hits the night before as Danny Mills in his dream. Of course, his mother was only teasing. She couldn't know about his dreams of The Wonder Kid or any of the other characters whose lives he escaped into while he slept. This was just the small talk she made each morning to distract him from what could be the embarrassment of being manhandled. His mom was amazing that way.

Before he would even realize what was happening, she had straightened out Cooper's legs and arms and taken off his clothes. She'd changed the small colostomy bag that was attached to him via tubes. Of course, he couldn't go to the bathroom on his own. He couldn't even feel the sensation of having to go. The tubes and bags did the job for him, and April would change them, and clean Cooper as needed. Then, she'd pull up his sheet again, leave the room, turning on his favorite music on the way out and, when she returned, she would sponge bathe him and simultaneously rub his muscles. She looked Cooper in the eye the whole time and spoke about things that interested him, or things that didn't, like the happenings in the lives of people his mother knew but who weren't really in his life. Either way, she distracted him and the next thing he knew she would be pulling on his daytime clothing.

That was the thing about Cooper's mom. She never made a production of having to coddle and nurse her son. She treated him as normally as he imagined other mothers treated their normal sons.

"Guess what," she said as she pulled him into a hug toward her and she began to massage Cooper's back.

"I've been clipping some of the online coupons. Maybe we could plan a shopping day with Uncle Harry soon and we'll all go to lunch and get haircuts."

"Not cutting my hair, mom."

"I tried," she laughed. "Well, at least the new clothes then. I swear you've grown four inches in the last month."

"Sounds good," Cooper choked out. His voice was already beginning to sound better.

His mom returned him gently to a laying position and then activated the bed lift to raise him to a near seated position while she picked out his clothes.

"Not that one," Cooper said as she showed him a t-shirt featuring a character from his favorite comic book. "Makes me look washed out."

"Washed out," she shook her head while putting it back. "When did you become so fashion-conscious?"

"Oh, by all means, put me those white leather tennis shoes that belong on eighty-year-old candy stripers and be sure to pair them with some no-elastic men's black business socks."

"Cut that out," she scolded him.

Cooper's mother knew that he was talking about one of the other kids his age at the rehab facility where he received physical therapy. The boy wore whatever the facility donated to his family and, since some clothing required modifying, those donations rarely had style in mind.

"You should be ashamed making such a comment. Your care would be very expensive if you didn't have your aunt and I to help. Some people in your position would be grateful with half of what you have," she said, while pulling on his clothing.

He didn't like this t-shirt, either, but knew better to say anything. He may not be rolling down a runway, but the outfit would have had him blending in like any other teenager. Granted, he didn't exactly look like Danny Mills, The Wonder Kid, either.

Cooper's skin, short of his face, was very fair, having rarely seen the sun over the last eight years. His eyes were hazel, like his mom's. His body was soft, as opposed to muscular and, since he was never seen standing, he was hardly ever considered to be tall. That considered, his mom was right. The pants were beginning to have a highwater look about them.

Coop wondered if he actually was tall compared to other guys his age. His knees were a bit on the knobby side, but he wasn't skin-and-bones, either. His hair didn't have that shine and thickness of sun and sport like Danny Mills. He had brown hair that went about eight different directions on the top of his head. If it were up to his mom and uncle, it would be high and tight. Coop caught a glimpse of himself in his mirror as his mom finished dressing him, and he wondered what it would be like to have an athletic build and a sweat-soaked head of waves like The Wonder Kid.

"I'll grab your chair, son," she said. "Do you want to stay up or lie back down."

"Up," he said, his voice at last sounding like a normal sixteen-year-old.

His mom winked at him as she got his chair ready.

He stayed there, of course, waiting. His mattress was mostly upright against the simple, hospital style headboard. A pillow was behind him, and his legs were stretched out before him on the bed. His mom turned off the motorized bed-sore preventors and retrieved the wheelchair from across the room. They had a routine for this, too.

Cooper's mom, April, was not a particularly large woman. She was barely over five feet tall and always wore her dark hair in short, unruly curls. She rarely wore makeup or perfume because she said she had no need for such frills. April had tiny high cheekbones, thin pink lips, and a perfect button nose. Around the house, she was usually in tank tops and shorts with flip flops or slip-on tennis shoes. April was strong from years of working with her son, though. As he grew, day-by-day, so her strength seemed to, as well.

Any presumed frailty based on April's appearance was shattered when you saw her slide Cooper effortlessly into his chair. She would pull the wheelchair up to the bed and slide Cooper to the edge. Then, lifting him at the middle with her shoulder, she would hoist him into his chair. She gently rolled his upper body against the back of his chair and shifted him into the center of the seat. She would tighten straps over his waist and chest. April had to put Cooper's hands in place next, on the arms of the chair. Ensuring that all of the settings on his chair were set for stability, she'd move to his feet. She would massage and put pressure on the soles of his feet to keep them strong before putting on orthopedic shoes that ensured proper shape. She squeezed his foot into them today.

"Looks like you may get some of those white leather shoes, after all, kid," she said, giving him a teasing glare. "Your feet are growing even faster than the rest of you."

Cooper jokingly stuck his tongue out at her as she placed his feet onto the footrests and pulled soft straps over them, as well as his arms. Last, she pushed a button on his chair that performed similar air-pressure transfers in the cushion and back of the chair as the air tubes in his bed's mattress did. He didn't have it on at all times, but the therapists recommend he use it routinely.

His wheelchair was very advanced, even beyond the sore-preventing chambers. After April placed her son's head in the pillow-padded headrest that kept him from looking like what he called a Cooper Ridge Bobble Head, she pulled a tiny remote control up to his mouth. It was something like a joystick, only very small. When he wore it, he looked like he was wearing one of those microphones that pop singers had on when they did concerts.

At first, the independence of moving from a manual chair to a remote control in his own power was overwhelming to Cooper, but he soon grew to love the freedom he had in his latest chair. Cooper was a pro at operating his joystick. He would use his lips, teeth, and tongue to move the remote. That was how he controlled his wheelchair's movements. He prided himself on the ability to make turns as quickly and accurately as those he knew who could operate their chairs by hand.

"Do you want to be pushed or do you want to remote?" asked April.

"Pushed for now," said Cooper.

His mouth was still dry before morning breakfast and it sometimes made working his chair on his own difficult. Even the metallic taste bothered him as the first thing to touch his tastebuds.

After they ate was usually when April would brush her son's teeth. Cooper didn't like the way toothpaste made his food taste, either. April agreed to hold off on brushings until after her shower and before his schooling.

April pushed her only child down the long hallway, past the closet full of his disability supplies. They affectionately referred to the closet as the hospital gift shop. Many of the items within it were donated by the doctors, nurses, and others who had cared for Cooper in those first two years after the accident during which nobody was sure he'd ever be able to go home at all. There were all sorts of physical therapy items and aids. There was also tech like dictation machines, audio books, and other things to make a disabled life more enjoyable. Most of the tech had become obsolete with voice-to-text tablets and smartphones. Also in the closet though, were oxygen tanks and tubes should Cooper ever need to be hooked up to a ventilator again.

Ventilator times were frightening times. Those were the times when people who called themselves nurses came to help his mom. Except Cooper knew they weren't just "regular" nurses. They were part of hospice teams, preparing for a presumed impending death.

The hospice visits had happened twice in Cooper's life. Once when he'd gotten pneumonia and once when April, feeling sick herself, had collapsed with Cooper. She couldn't in her own weakened state get him off the floor and, in her attempts to do so, she'd managed to crack one of his ribs. The incident had taken place in the first few months after he had been released to the home and his mom was still learning how to manage movement of her son. After the fall, his aunt came to help until April was ready to be alone again. She always had the strength. She just needed training and support . . . and the time necessary to get over her fear of hurting Cooper again.

Most quadriplegics needed a great deal of specialty equipment like that which was in the gift shop – like the ventilators. Cooper was lucky to have had a special pacemaker of sorts implanted to help his diaphragm continue expanding and contracting to breathe normally. Oxygen was only required in emergency circumstances.

As April continued pushing Coop down the hall, they passed her room in which she had her own bathroom, then they rolled beyond a second bathroom with a special shower for Cooper that could be closed and filled as a hot tub of sorts with massaging jets. There was also a handicapped toilet, although it didn't really get use. It had been installed when he was still in an induced coma after the accident, and they had hopes he might not be permanently paralyzed. Instead, the colostomy bag bio-disposal can in the bathroom was used and a home service came and picked up the bio-trash twice a week.

A turn at the end of the hallway to the kitchen came next. Past the eat-in kitchen and pantry was a living room with a television and then, a home office. A door on one side of the office led to a staircase down to the basement. Cooper hadn't been there since before the accident. At one time, they were going to install a special riding chair that attached to the railing, but there wasn't really a reason for him to go down there, so it was never a priority. He remembered roller skating on the hard floors of the lower level when he was a boy, but that wasn't going to be happening again.

To the other side of the kitchen was Cooper's study room. It had once been an enclosed porch but was converted for his school needs. It contained a table-like desk and there was a projector. His homework tools, many and varied, were kept there so that he could use them almost completely independent of assistance. He was tutored in that room and—on one side—there was a large open space with mats lain down and exercise machines on which he would receive daily physical therapy.

When they got to the kitchen, Cooper's mom parked him at the low counter and proceeded to make her coffee.

"You feeling up to solids today?" April questioned her son.

"No," he said.

Cooper's solid foods were not really solid the way most people have; steaks were never on the menu. Once, in a fancy restaurant, he was able to eat a bite of filet mignon that was tender enough for him to enjoy. He remembered it melting in his mouth. Within the daily routine though, solid food meant he would attempt scrambled eggs and cooked vegetables, or—when he was really lucky—banana cream pie. He loved bananas. More often than not, his solid breakfast consisted of a thin oatmeal or cream of wheat with some sort of fruit puree mixed into it to cover the taste of his powdered supplements.

Coop was luckier than some quadriplegics if that could be a thing. His paralysis began below his neck and throat, just above his heart and lungs. Technically, the tops of his shoulders weren't without feeling, but moving shoulders when you can't move the joints to which they are attached, was an impossibility. However, he was able to feel food in his mouth, swallow, and even appreciate the senses of the swallowed bits going down . . . until they disappeared into the numb abyss that was his body. Nonetheless, eating various solids required a lot of help and a lot of time.

He nearly choked one time and was lucky that his Uncle Harry had been there. In the midst of he and his mom panicking, Cooper was tossing his own head about, and April was unsuccessfully trying to fish the food out of her son's throat. His Uncle had run into the room, assessed the situation, taken in his options, leapt across the room, and punched Cooper in the diaphragm just beneath his ribs. With that, a chunk of banana launched out of Coop's mouth across the room.

"What the hell, Harry?" April screamed.

Cooper's eyes were watering, but he was breathing, his head hanging low out of the pillow rest while he caught his breath.

"I didn't know else to do!" he yelled back.

"I'm good, Mom," Cooper managed at last. "I'm good."

As crazy as it was, Uncle Harry's makeshift Heimlich maneuver was a lot easier than quickly wrestling Cooper out of the wheelchair and attempting to perform the lifesaving method in the more traditional manner on the boy's limp body.

In time, the story became their family's too-often-repeated inside joke. Uncle Harry would walk into the kitchen punching one fist into his other palm and ask, "So what's for dinner, tonight, Coop? Rocketing Ragu? Projectile pea soup? Shooting shellfish?" or any other random alliteration he was able to concoct.

Most of Cooper's meals could be taken through a straw. April tried very hard to keep them exciting and varied so that Cooper didn't get bored. She made sure the meals were healthy not just for her son's sake but also to help keep her job of cleaning up after the digestion as easy as possible. This morning, he had blended yogurt and banana; it was a delicious day. His mom threw in a couple of crushed graham crackers, too. April stayed in the room while he drank his breakfast smoothie in case there was a problem. Then, after giving him some water, she turned on a small television screen on the counter so that Cooper could watch his favorite morning show while she left to shower and dress for the day.

Chapter 4

School

C ooper had classes year-round. He thought it was a pretty bum deal. All the work and almost none of the socializing.

Sure, he had the youth rehab group, but some of them were half his age, so he didn't have much in common with them other than disability. That seemed like a crappy connection at best. He remembered his aunt saying something similar when she had gone through and beaten breast cancer. There was a whole group of women who had bonded over their shared cancer diagnoses, and they had nothing else that made them friends. As some moved out of treatment, they lost touch, only to sadly come together again when one, and then another, eventually lost her battle to the disease. Coop hated the idea of growing close to and then possibly losing people with whom he had no real shared interests to begin with. Another bum deal, in his opinion.

Cooper had a private tutor that came to his home during the day. He had reading, writing, and arithmetic; he had science, social studies, and specials. His music and art classes were more about identifying and appreciating than it was about applying. He did try to sing sometimes, but not being able to feel his own lungs and diaphragm made it difficult at best to breathe optimally for singing. He was pretty sure he wouldn't be auditioning for an opera any time soon. He also tried painting while holding the brush in his teeth.

One girl at the rehab center was a part of a worldwide mouth painting organization. Yes. That really existed. She was amazing. The same couldn't be said for Coop. The organization wouldn't be chasing him down to join them. When he managed not to drop the brushes, his very best works resembled weak Jackson Pollock knockoffs that were tossed into a blender before being launched into a tornado that then dropped them in a lake to be fished out before being put onto somebody's wall.

For Cooper it was sports that got his blood pumping. Twice a month, he got to go the pool with his Uncle Harry for mobility exercises. He wore flotation devices, and he could almost imagine he was really swimming as his limbs moved fluidly through the deep. He remembered swimming from before the accident. He used to lay still, face down in the waters, holding his breath for as long as he could. Funny that the thing which was once like playing dead was actually what made him feel most alive today.

Besides "swimming," Coop enjoyed learning about the sports he didn't dare have the hope of playing. Hockey, football, soccer, basketball and—his favorite—baseball. Man, did he love baseball. He could talk stats for hours with his tutor. The idea of being a statistician or probability analyst was not an impossibility. On that, he did occasionally dare to dream. He could picture himself in the dugout of a World Series MLB team when they rushed the field. They would pick him up out of his chair and rush the field with him because he was part of the team. At least that's how he imagined it could go.

Several times a day, April would come in and clean Cooper up and give him a break from the learning, especially on a nice day. Sometimes the afternoon would move the learning outdoors or, on a particularly lucky day, he might go for a long drive and get to hear an audiobook or stream a video for his coursework. He used voice-to-text tools, special reading machines, and other devices to help him learn, too.

All of Coop's classes were taught by a private tutor named Derek Lowell. He was strict; he arrived precisely on time each day and kept a tight schedule similar to the block system used by students in the public schools. He had a master's degree in special education and was a self-acclaimed gym bro to boot, so he was fully capable of handling Cooper's rather heavy and bulky chair if April needed an assist.

After the day his mom had collapsed with him, there was a period of several months when, little by little, April had built a community to help with the needs of Cooper. The medical team was already in place.

Next, she'd brought in her sister, May, and May's husband, Harry. There was the psychologist Dr. Kahn she went to regularly to help her own mental well-being; occasionally Cooper would go with her. There were reliable neighbors and friends to support her and to befriend Cooper. The ones who stuck around, Nicholas and April, weren't those who saw their friendships as charity. They really liked Coop. And, finally, there was Mr. Lowell. He came on when Coop was starting middle school. The insurance money from after the accident had long been expended and she needed to work to make ends meet.

Besides, homeschooling became more and more difficult the older and more complex Cooper's studies became. There were subjects in which Cooper had an interest which just weren't topics his mother ever had to learn. She had taken French in high school, and he was interested in learning Spanish. He was interested in statistics and economics while she was more knowledgeable in physics and biology. The best education he could get was going to require somebody with a broader educational background. So, enter Mr. Lowell.

The tutor surprised Cooper. Knowing that he was a special educator, Coop expected softball treatment. In reality, Mr. Lowell was relatively hard on Cooper. He made clear from the start that he expected Cooper to know the same things as the "normal" kids in public school. There were no exceptions for his mind just because he had limitations in his body. "Limitations." That's what Mr. Lowell called them. It was a better word to Coop than "needs," as it was something that Mr. Lowell said everybody had. Cooper's just happened to be physical.

As opposed to the pass that many gave Cooper in his life as they felt sorry for him, Mr. Lowell drove Cooper to begin imagining aspects of adult independence. In addition to his studies, the two would weekly read research on advancements being made in paralysis treatment and management. For a field trip of sorts, Mr. Lowell had even taken Cooper to a high-tech research facility for wounded veterans. They connected Coop to an assortment of robotic pieces and electrodes while he stood—stood!—on a treadmill and, for a little bit, Cooper actually got to walk while his hands—or at least the robotic attachments to his hands—actually gripped the stabilizing bars on the sides of the treadmill. A technician stood at the side of the machine with hands on Coop's torso while he watched in amazement as his legs moved forward. Of course, it's not as though

Cooper's own body was doing the work, but it was exciting to see a future of possibilities with every step.

As if that day could have gotten any better, Mr. Lowell took Cooper to a baseball game afterward. That part of the trip was homework. Coop was required to keep stats during the gameplay. His tutor insisted that the soul needed dreams like those of being able to walk one day, but reality required a sharp mind to live in a world that may not achieve those dreams in his lifetime. He voice-to-texted existing batting averages and, in his head, calculated new highs and lows based on each pitch and swing.

Following the game, once the team's statistician gave Cooper a perfect score on his work, he led him through the tunnel behind the dugout to the team locker room. One of the players presented Cooper with a bat and said it was his to use *"when he got better one day."* The news crews there to get post-game reports ate that up. Cooper smiled even while he thought the guy was an idiot for saying he could get better. That's one of those stupid things people would say when they intended to be thoughtful and encouraging to him before they even realized the reality of his condition.

That night, when Mr. Lowell brought Cooper home, Coop said the bat was lame. But he had his mother rest it against his windowsill nonetheless, one of the places he could easily see from his bed.

Mr. Lowell was all-in-all an okay guy. There was no special attention on account of Cooper's special needs when it came to his studies; no shortcomings allowed below the neck. He promised Coop's mom a 4.0 in any area he was tasked with teaching. In short, Coop loved him.

So, for the past two years, did his mom. It took so long for April to date and, when she finally did so, a few years after his dad had died, the couple of guys that made it to the Cooper introduction had all been jerks. One spoke to him like a toddler. One seemed to think Cooper couldn't hear or see, so he'd speak about his condition right in front of him in pseudo-intellectual terms like some cereal box therapist. Another tried so hard to pretend that everything was normal that he would attempt to book impossible dates like hikes in the rock formations because he wanted to prove that he could manage Coop in any situation. April of course wanted a loving man who considered her son, but she couldn't tolerate a complete idiot.

Derek Lowell was different. He was a friend first and didn't try to win over April. Their relationship built more naturally over time. And an idiot he was not. He wasn't just good for Cooper. His mom was well-treated, too. One night, he even saw Mr. Lowell and his mom dancing. The same guy who was a hardass on him in his studies and who was a gym rat loved to make April feel special by spinning her around in the kitchen.

Dancing may have been out of the question for Cooper, but he did actually have to have physical education of sorts beyond what Mr. Lowell could bring. Each day ended the same way, with his mom's sister, his Aunt May, coming to help with is physical therapy. Cooper always thought his grandparents on his mom's side must have had a great sense of humor. His mom, who was born in the month of May, was named April, and her sister, born in April, was named May.

Cooper's Aunt and mother couldn't look more different. Where April was tiny and petite, May was tall and muscle-bound. April was typically in shorts and tank tops and May was in jeans and flannels, even in the summer when she might at best replace the flannel with a t-shirt. Both women had beautiful smiles, though, and Cooper was warmed by his aunt's presence when she entered a room.

Aunt May was a nurse, and she was a blessing for Cooper and his mother. Without her, they probably couldn't afford the sort of personal care he needed, much less could they get it every day. Plus, she was married to Cooper's Uncle Harry who was just an added bonus. Uncle Harry did construction work and always made sure buildings were accessible. He often joined on daytrips, too, when Mr. Lowell could not. That way, his chair could be carried in those places that didn't have his stamp of accessibility approval.

"Hey Coop," his Aunt May said at the end of the day when she arrived. "You ready for a hardcore workout today?"

"I don't really see the point, Aunt May," he grumbled. "I was planning on holding off on that miraculous recovery," he added, attempting a joke to cover up his accidental negativity; Aunt May was insistent on positive energy in her physical therapy space.

"We've talked about this more times than I can count," she began, not letting him get away with the slip. "In your case," she went on as she took his blood pressure, temperature, and resting pulse, "It's not about trying to regain movement. It's about trying to keep your muscles strong enough to protect your body and about keeping your circulation healthy."

Cooper stopped himself from rolling his eyes. His aunt stretched and bent and twisted and massaged his arms and his legs. She turned his feet and hands at the joints and ran his legs by bending his knees like a bicycle. She'd push the soles of his feet against different blocks of wood, rubber foam, and other materials to keep them strong and properly shaped.

Half of the time, Cooper stayed in his chair and half of the time was spent on the floor mats. Once a week, he'd also get a massage while on his stomach on a padded massage table that allowed his face to peek out through a hole to breathe. Aunt May was good at what she did, but not good at hiding the fact that she was doing it. As grateful as he was for her help, he always felt a bit ridiculous during physical therapy. He'd grown used to it over the years, but it was the time of day when he most was reminded of his inabilities.

His aunt took his pulse again and then put down her wristwatch-laden hand in frustration. "That's strange. Okay, before I take all of your vitals again, I'm going to put you on the autos."

"But it's Monday!" complained Cooper.

The autos were the nickname Aunt May gave to refer to any of the machines to which she would attach Cooper. He sat in them or laid on them while the machine would lift and bend his arms and legs on its own. He felt more like a robot than a man on the autos. He was prisoner to the commands his aunt had pre-entered to provide his cardio workout. He tolerated the exercise in circulation and humiliation because he usually only had to do them on Tuesdays and Thursdays, plus one weekend morning with his mom.

"I know. But usually, oh-so-strong-nephew-of-mine, your heart rate rises from the physical therapy. Today it hasn't. So, I want to exercise you a little bit more before I check your stats again."

She spoke to Cooper in directives as she hooked and strapped his arms and legs onto the foam paddles that would lift his various appendages.

"Fine," he huffed, as though he were giving her permission to do what she had already done.

"I'm glad you approve, Dr. Cooper!" she joked. "I've set it for fifteen minutes. I'm going to talk to my sister for a bit."

"I won't go anywhere," was his snarky response.

May looked back to scold him but Cooper was smiling wryly, showing he had only sassed for her reaction.

Chapter 5

A Growing Boy

xcept for the times that April helped to clean up Cooper or change his colostomy bags (which were kept discreetly in a black Velcro pouch at the back of his wheelchair, while the tubes were concealed in black elastic wraps beneath his attire), she made herself scarce during the day so that Mr. Lowell and Aunt May could do their work. April ran a small online business from home, reselling cleaned up and refurbished items found at garage sales and thrift stores. Other than runs to find items or trips to the post office, she did most of her work out of a workshop and photo studio in the basement. She was around if needed, but not a disturbance for Cooper if she didn't have to be.

When Aunt May arrived for physical therapy, Mr. Lowell would visit with April for a little bit before leaving. The sounds in the home managed to bounce around so freely that the basement was almost like a whisper room where even quietly spoken words would travel up the stairs straight to Cooper's ears. He was not appreciative, especially when the words would stop, and he heard the unpleasant smacking of kisses. Wanting his mom to be in love was one thing. Wanting to hear it was quite another.

May didn't particularly look forward to having to intrude, either, but it seemed the words were still flowing today, so she didn't hesitate.

"Hey Derek, how are you?" she asked Mr. Lowell when she'd reached the bottom of the stairs.

Cooper tuned in as well as he could over the whirring buzz of the autos.

"Good! Great day. You?"

"I don't want to interrupt," she said.

Cooper's mom shook her head. "What's with the formalities? Something going on?" she asked her sister.

"It's nothing, I'm sure. But . . . well . . . Cooper," she began at a loss for words.

"What about him?" April's tone immediately swapped to one of concern.

"It's not a bad thing. Let me sit," she added, still not sure of herself or even her reason for the conversation that she had begun.

Cooper heard the squeaking that indicated his aunt was fidgeting in the chair before standing back up. He heard her soft shoes begin their pacing. Cooper recognized her voice growing louder and then quieter as she passed in front of the stairs back and forth and back and forth. His autos continued to whisper over her voice.

"Have you been doing the regular routines with him lately?" his aunt asked his mom. "Same exercises? Same vitamins and medications? Nothing strenuous?"

"Sure. I mean," she paused. Cooper could picture his mother's thinking face. "Yes. Yes, I have. I'm not sure what you are trying to get at, but nothing has changed around here. I'm certainly not pushing him," April added almost defensively.

"It's not that," May reassured her.

"Is. He. Okay?" April asked with deliberate pause.

"Yes. He's okay. But there's something I've noticed for a while now."

"What is it?" Mr. Lowell chimed in.

"This is going to sound ridiculous. But Cooper's muscles are becoming. Ugh. This is just strange." May fumbled.

April was impatient. "WHAT?"

"They're becoming developed," May finally finished.

After a pause, Mr. Lowell asked, "That's good, isn't it?"

"It's great," Aunt May exclaimed. "It's just nonsensical."

"He's sixteen, sis'," April said.

"I know he is. And yes, growth happens at sixteen and beyond and before. But this isn't normal. I mean, it would be normal for a normal body, but not a paralyzed one. It's not just Cooper's muscles. It's his heart rate, too. His resting pulse is fabulous. Today I couldn't even get him up to a target heart rate."

"You're just doing a great job," April said.

"I wish I could take the credit. His cardiovascular system is like that of an athlete and yes. It is a good thing. I just don't understand it. Most people as severely limited as Cooper, especially from an accident as opposed to from birth, they have a certain limit on life."

Mr. Lowell cut in, "May—"

"Don't stop me. You know what I say is true, Derek. So do you, April. I'm not talking about the value of life. I'm talking about the length of life. The body does not stay healthy when it is forced to be idle for so long. Human bodies are not made to be still. Muscles begin to break down. The heart grows weak from lack of exerting its strength. The lungs even grow weak from the lack of necessity of them to fill to capacity."

Cooper could hear that his aunt had stopped pacing. If he were to guess, his mom was the one in the chair now and her sister was crouched before her to have the serious talk with a dose of compassion. It was the position he'd seen her take in the hospital when May told her that her son wouldn't walk again. It was the position she'd taken after the fall when she told April she needed to get some help. He didn't need to be in the room to know that's where Aunt May was now.

"If I knew of Cooper's situation but didn't know the boy, I would say he's lucky to still be alive. He's beaten the odds but now those odds of him making it even longer in a healthy way are against him," May sighed.

"But you just said," Cooper's mother interjected.

"That he's doing great," May finished for her sister. "He is. That is what I'm saying. I've been a nurse and therapist for as many years as he's been around. I've worked in therapy with wounded and paralyzed patients for twelve of those years and eight of them with my nephew. I've never seen something like this. Cooper is as healthy as any sixteen-year-old, healthier than some of them! I just wish I understood why. There is no logical explanation for his strength and endurance or for the athletic condition of his body."

"Oh," April said, unsure of how she should respond.

Derek contributed equal confusion. "Are we sorry?"

"No! Of course not," May said. "I'm just looking for answers and thought one of you might have something is all. An idea. I don't know why Cooper is so unusual. I wish I did. Hell, the entire medical community would wish to know his magic formula. He's getting better, April."

Cooper wished the autos would stop their humming. The conversation was growing quieter, and he didn't want to miss a word, or worse, mishear one. He swore that his aunt said he was getting better. His mind flashed back to the robotic walking on the treadmill except he pictured himself on it without any of the mechanical attachments, without somebody holding up his body at the torso. He dared, for an instant, to have hope. If his aunt had desired to increase his heartrate, that image would surely suffice to do so.

"I'm not saying Coop could move or even, I don't know, dream of it. His nerves are still not making connections, but his body thinks that it has done so. It thinks it has moved. It's strong."

Everyone was quiet.

"Well, if you ladies won't say it, can I?" Mr. Lowell's smile could be heard in his voice. "Even though we don't know the answer, can we just be selfishly happy that it is happening with our boy?"

Cooper smiled too, hearing his tutor refer to him as "his boy." The autos let out a beeping sound and slowed to a stop.

"That's the end of the workout, April. Let me see if your son actually has a target heart rate, yet." Added Aunt May before making her way back up the stairs to Cooper the robot.

His aunt took his vitals once last time and his physical therapy was officially over. His mother cleaned him up and he went to watch a program while his mom prepared dinner for him, her, and Mr. Lowell who occasionally (and more and more often) joined them.

Cooper's only "chore" that he could do was to program the automatic vacuum. He took pride in doing it because it made him feel like he was contributing to the house. It had become simple for him, though, so he could program the machine and watch television at the same time.

"Don't fry your brain on a mindless show," Mr. Lowell said, his teacherly tone laid on heavily.

"If I had a better tutor, he'd make sure my brain was fry-proof," Cooper joked back.

He knew what the man really thought of him, but no need to get mushy.

Chapter 6

Mr. Lowell's Loss For Words

After dinner, Cooper started on his homework. He had to watch a documentary on penguins and complete some voice-to-text Spanish translations. His mom and Mr. Lowell did the dishes. A short while into the documentary, Mr. Lowell came in to join Cooper in the living room where he was working.

"How about we sit out on the porch, Cooper?" he asked. "It's a cool night out there."

"My tutor may not want me to stop doing my homework," he jibed.

"Come on, kid. Remote on out here."

Cooper actually wasn't feeling up to remoting at that time, but Mr. Lowell wasn't planning on coming to his aid, so he told the television to turn off by voice command and he took himself, careful not to run into the automatic floor vacuum, to the specially mounted pad on the wall where he spoke a code out loud, and the front door swung open. It was a wider door than most homes, specifically installed to allow for the width of his chair. He rolled over the seamless mound between the inside of the house and the outdoor porch.

The air that night was warm and thick with the scent of the desert shrubbery and red clay stone they had in place of a green lawn. Cooper did love the way the evening air settled around him at that perfect time just before the fireflies began to make their lighted nightly appearances, complete with a choreographed candlelit performance. He could close his eyes and feel the tingle of warmth blend with the occasional cool brushing of a breeze about his face. He imagined what it would be like to experience that sensation through to the very tips of his fingers and toes – his every nerve alive and dancing with the splendor of an end-of-summer-dusk-time atmosphere. Cooper took a deep breath and smiled.

"You really do look well, tonight, Coop," Mr. Lowell said.

"I am well," he returned.

Mr. Lowell plopped into the front porch swing, but he didn't look like he actually wanted to be sitting. He put one foot up on a knee. Then, he switched. Then he put both feet on the ground and leaned forward. He parted his lips as if about to say something but closed them again before actually speaking. Then, he leaned back and spread himself wide across the seat, pushing his back against the slats of the porch bench and laying one arm across it.

"Fidget much?" Coop asked with a furrowed brow.

After a sigh, "Can't seem to get comfortable," the tutor said with a fluster.

Cooper didn't provide any relief and in fact seemed to enjoy seeing the man squirm. He thought he knew what might be coming.

"We've known each other a long time, haven't we?" he began, and Cooper was completely unaccustomed to this rather timid conversational route from his tutor.

"Yeah."

"Yes," Mr. Lowell corrected, some of his teaching automation slipping through.

"Yes," said Cooper begrudgingly.

"I don't have any kids of my own," the older man went on. "Of course, you already know this. And I don't have a wife. Well, of course you already know that. I mean, I . . . I've been . . . well, you know your mom and I date."

"Gross," Cooper said.

Mr. Lowell stood up abruptly and asked, "Why don't we walk? I'll push."

"Sure," Cooper said.

Mr. Lowell took up the wheelchair handles from behind Cooper and led him off the porch down the back-and-forth twisting wheelchair ramp that the boy's uncle had built. He led Coop first to the driveway and then to the sidewalk beyond.

"It's a beautiful night," the man said.

"Pretty sure we've covered that," said Coop.

"The thing is, Cooper," proceeded Mr. Lowell as he pushed the teen down the walk of the neighborhood, "I really like your mom."

Not making this any easier, "Yep. Covered that, too," Cooper chimed in.

"Well, and, if you don't know how much I also care about you by now, then I am doing something very wrong," said Mr. Lowell.

This one actually caught Cooper off-guard a bit. I mean, sure, they were close. But they didn't actually say those things out loud. Still, it was a lot easier to crack wise than get sentimental.

"I guess you're doing something wrong, then!" he joked.

The chair stopped moving.

"Are you— I— What . . . but—" Mr. Lowell stumbled.

"Kidding!" Cooper said smiling.

"You little shit!" the tutor said as he began pushing again; but finally, he seemed like himself once more.

"Ooh, I'm telling Mom!"

"She'd agree," he laughed.

"Probably," said Coop.

"I just wanted to say that when three people are around one another as much as the three of us are, they're kind of already a family, aren't they?"

"Yeah."

"Well, what if I want to be around even more? Like, what if I want to be around all the time and if your mom says yes . . . "

"Are you asking for my blessing?" Cooper asked with a tone that he tried to make silly, but his voice cracked in the midst of it like he was prepubescent.

Ignoring the preteen squeak that had given away Cooper's real emotions, "Yes. Yes, I am. I wanted to make sure you were okay with it before I asked her. And I kind of already have the ring."

"Weren't you confident?" Cooper joked.

"And I'm sort of impatient."

Cooper laughed. Mr. Lowell came to a stop in front of the home of a neighbor and he looked down at Cooper.

"What do you think?" he asked as he crouched in front of the wheelchair and looked the young man in the eyes.

Cooper just nodded. There was a lump in his throat, and he didn't want to give himself away. He blinked his eyes to make sure he didn't end up crying.

Once he swallowed back his emotions, Cooper managed, "You got it, Mr. Lowell. She'll say yes. I'm sure."

"And that Mr. Lowell stuff will have to go away. Maybe just Derek."

"Sure, Derek," said Cooper and then he immediately wrinkled his nose. "Ooh. That will take some getting used to."

"We've got a lifetime," said Derek as he put a hand on each side of Cooper's face. It wasn't a hug, but it meant even more because he knew that Cooper could feel it. The two glowed happily and the tutor may even have been ready to hug the teen for real but—just then—Hank Rutherford came out to his front yard with his son Nicholas and their dog, Beaches.

Chapter 7

The Neighbor's Memory

"**H**ey Derek!" called Mr. Rutherford. "Great night, huh?"

"Yes. Yes, it is!" Derek exclaimed in deliberate announcement as though he were feeling this had just been confirmed.

Cooper smiled at him as his tutor stood and turned toward Hank.

"Perfect Arizona weather," Mr. Rutherford added.

Nodding, Derek went on with, "Supposed to get a bit cool come Thursday."

Well, that did it. Cooper was bored. What was it with adults and talking about the weather? And worse than that, no matter where in the country they lived or were from, they all thought the conversation was completely unique to them. *Well, you know in Arizona, we always talk about the weather,* his Uncle Harry said on a worksite. He had a cousin in Maryland who joked, *Well, that's Maryland weather for you. You wouldn't get it.* And his grandparents who had been from Wisconsin? They could go on for an hour recounting the years of snowless Christmases and the ones that had them snowed in and unable to leave; the Januaries with windchill temperatures in the negative fifties; and the summers with stretches over a hundred degrees. Whenever Cooper found himself with a need to take the spotlight off of him in a roomful of adults, all he had to do was mention something ambivalent about the weather and, guaranteed, the conversation would take off, and he could take off remoting away to another room.

For now, Cooper looked toward the house for his friend.

"What are you up to tonight?" Derek asked.

"Nicky has some new trick he's doing with Beaches he wanted to show off to me," his neighbor said proudly. "Come on up, you two. We'll come down off the porch for Cooper."

Nicholas and Beaches bounded down their wooden porch steps with Mr. Rutherford behind while Mr. Lowell pushed Cooper up their front walk.

"Hey Coop!" said Nicholas.

"How you doin', son?" said Mr. Rutherford. He patted Cooper on the head in the same way he'd pat Beaches. "Nice to get out in the fresh air, isn't it?"

Cooper took a deep, calming breath and, before he could say anything in return, Mr. Lowell cut in.

"So, what's this new trick of your son's?"

Derek could tell that Cooper was uncomfortable. It wasn't that Mr. Rutherford was mean to Cooper. He just didn't seem to understand that he was a sixteen-year-old guy, the same age as his own son. Yet Coop had heard him speak to Nicholas as though he was completely grown.

Nicholas, on the other hand, who had known Cooper his whole life and been over to play video games countless times through the years, was just the opposite. He did not know that he should treat Cooper differently than anyone else.

"I'll show you guys," Nicholas shared, his huge white smile shining brightly between his dark lips. "But Coop, hey! I got a new game and it's a joystick one and you can use the joystick that has a button in the middle of the top I think, and I tried it without my hands and I'm not very good but you're obviously better at that than me and maybe you could come by and try it," his friend finished in a single breath.

"Cool," Cooper smiled back, a man of far fewer words.

"Well, we'll see if that's something he can handle," Mr. Rutherford added with another pat on the head.

Cooper steamed, but Derek placed a gentle hand on his shoulder to calm him.

"How about this trick of yours, Nicky?" Mr. Lowell prompted.

"Oh yeah. Coop! Watch this! It is so cool!"

Nicholas pulled out a yo-yo and began to get it started up and down the string. Then, he turned to his sandy colored dog. As he rolled the yo-yo down, Beaches laid flat on the ground. When the yo-yo came up, Beaches would stand. Up and down, up and down went the yo-yo . . . and the dog, too.

"Isn't that awesome!" Nicholas said excitedly. "Here, you do it!" he said bringing the yo-yo to Cooper and putting the string into his mouth with the ease of somebody who had done it many times.

Cooper didn't feel much like doing it, but his friend's enthusiasm was so sincere and hard to deny. Nicholas was his one truest and closest friend. The two would play video games together and even the occasional tabletop or roleplaying game with his friend moving a piece for Coop when necessary.

Nicholas loved playing at yo-yo tricks, too. He could do walk the dog and around the world and all sorts of other things Coop didn't know the names of. The year before—with a great deal of patience—he had taught Cooper how to do the simple up and down with the yo-yo. He'd put the string in Cooper's mouth after he had wound it tightly. Then, Cooper could make it go up and down several times if he jerked his head back at just the right time and managed to lean his head far enough over one side of the chair that his wheels and mechanics didn't get in the way. His friend had even given him his own very nice trick yo-yo. Cooper had once made the toy return eight times in a row and he probably could have done even more but, on that eighth snap up, the yo-yo hit Cooper a little too hard in the face and the string popped out of his mouth. The yo-yo fell to the ground, and something came loose in it that meant it was never able to be quite as tightly wound again. Cooper promised Nicholas he'd have his mom tighten it up and keep practicing, but he'd only gotten to it a couple of times before—much like the bat from the professional baseball player—the yo-yo found a resting place in his bedroom. It was on the nightstand next to his bed, just beneath the light of the bedside lamp.

"You ready for me to let go?" asked Nicholas as he held the toy at the corner of his friend's mouth.

"Uh-huh," Cooper responded through teeth gritted down onto the string.

Nicholas dropped the yo-yo as it fell from the pulley of Cooper's mouth. Beaches laid down. When Cooper felt the tug of the string, he jerked his head back to recall the yo-yo. It returned halfway. Beaches stood. The yo-yo then made another descent and Beaches laid down again. This time, Cooper yanked his head back too late, and the yo-yo only rose about an inch before simply spinning around at the bottom like a carnival swing. Beaches cocked his long-nosed face to one side, then rolled over onto his back and playfully twisted around on the grass beside the walkway.

"That's okay, boy," said Mr. Rutherford.

Cooper wasn't sure whether he meant him or the dog. He was a little embarrassed. Nicholas, however, was thrilled.

"COOL! You made him roll over! I wanna try!" he exclaimed, while grabbing the yo-yo from Cooper and attempting to repeat the spinning yo-yo that his friend had accomplished by accident.

The men continued in their conversation about things that didn't much interest Cooper; the new construction of nearby homes, some old tool store that closed in town, and bits and pieces about politics and other adult subjects that dared venture beyond the weather. Nicholas, meanwhile, was managing tricks with Beaches on the lawn and Cooper just took in the scene. He looked around the neighborhood and saw Ashley walking with her friend across the street, probably to the park at the end of the block.

Ashley looked like she was pretty enough to be in her twenties. At least in the eyes of Cooper who always looked younger than his own age. She was with him the day of the accident. They were just kids, of course, but their parents—before that day—had already had the girl-next-door and boy-next-door pair married off in the future. Ashley and he weren't technically next door to one another. She was across the street and a couple houses down. Still, their parents used to play card games at night and the two of them became playmates during those frequent evenings. Coop and Ashley were bosom buddies hanging out as toddlers, in elementary school, and even pretty routinely up until a few months after he was home from the hospital. Then not as much, mostly because her parents and his mom had grown apart. They still loved one another, but couple friends tend to be drawn to other couple friends and his mom was no longer part of a couple.

Ashley's folks went out a few times on double dates with his mom and Derek, and it seemed like they were growing closer again. It was a bonus for Cooper because sometimes Ashley would hang out at the house when the four of them went out. She would do her homework and was there basically to call if there was an emergency. But it wasn't babysitting. The two hung out and watched movies and talked.

After the accident, there had been so much attention around Cooper and his family. It lasted for months following the crash, and Coop had been so young, that he never had an opportunity or even the forethought to ask Ashley how she was affected by the day. He'd heard, years later, that Ashley couldn't go to the park for a very long time, and she had nightmares whenever the sound of some car rushing down the street made its way into her sleep. He never had to see the trauma; he was in it. Whatever she'd gone through, Ash had stuck around, visiting him in the hospital and rehab center, keeping him caught up on the news as news is for the eight- and then nine-year-olds they were at the time. Eventually, her visits became once a week, then once a month, and then just on occasion. These days, she visited usually a few times a year – on a holiday or, less importantly, on some random day when her friends were out of town, and she had nothing to do but stream a movie.

Ashley moved on, not that there was ever a negative between the two of them. They still got along and could talk and laugh together. They probably would have started growing apart during those middle school years. Cooper wondered though, if it hadn't been for the accident, maybe this is when they would have grown back together, perhaps even as a couple.

Ashley waved across the road to Cooper, and he blinked, before nodding as heavily as he could to indicate a "Hello" back to her. Then he turned back to Nicholas. He didn't realize he had been staring.

Beaches was continuing to go up and down to the rhythm of Nicholas's yo-yo and his friend praised the dog like the parent of a child taking her first steps.

"Now, try this," Nicholas began. He made the yo-yo spin at the bottom of the string. Beaches laid down. "Now, Beaches," said the boy. Beaches stood back up. "Not that, either" he said to his pet ruffling his head affectionately so that his "no" didn't upset the dog.

They practiced going up and down some more and, this time, when Nicholas got to the spinning yo-yo, he dropped it entirely and got on his own back on the ground like Beaches had earlier, twisting back and forth. Beaches didn't roll over though, to mimic his owner. Instead, he playfully pounced on Nicholas.

"Beaches!" Nicholas laughed.

The two rolled around in the yard while Nicholas chuckled and covered his face to protect it from Beaches' licking and gentle pawing. Nicholas was sixteen, good looking, popular, and an athlete. But with Beaches, he may as well have been the same giddy and goofy ten-year-old he had been when they first got the dog as a puppy. The continued to wrestle about, and Cooper couldn't help but laugh at the spectacle, too.

"Good boy, Beaches! Good boy!" Nicholas praised.

Then, from between the two of them, Cooper saw two fireflies appear seemingly out of nowhere. They were the brightest fireflies he had ever seen, and big, too—more like violet glowing stars—rising up to the sky. He closed his eyes. They'd have to go in, soon, and he wanted to enjoy this moment. When he reopened his eyes, he couldn't see the first fireflies, but throughout the night air, he began to notice the small flickering tails of the winged beacons of night appearing all around him.

"I guess we'd better call it a night, Derek," said Mr. Rutherford.

"Yes, yes," he said. "We'd better get walking back, too. Goodnight, Nicky," added Derek. "Great job with Beaches."

"Thanks, Mr. Lowell. See ya', Coop."

"Bye," said Cooper. He continued to listen as he was pushed away and the Rutherfords went indoors.

"Some trick, Nicky. Some trick. I think we'll have some ice cream before bed."

It was just a short while later that Cooper found himself tucked into his bed sheets for the night after his bedtime exercises were completed. His sleeping position was slightly varied from the night before as just one more precaution against pressure sores. His curtains were wide open with the window cracked to the sweet, still, desert air. Knowing that, just down the hall, Mr. Lowell . . . Derek . . . would soon be asking his mom to be his wife, Cooper smiled happily and closed his eyes.

The night began noiselessly but eventually the chirping of the crickets began to enter his dreams. At some point in that confused time between awake and asleep, he felt certain he heard, in place of the song of the desert crickets, tiny voices floating above him in his then dreamless sleep. Cooper dozily turned his head to one side and felt a fall tickle in the ear that was not against his pillow.

In an instant, Coop was running down a set of wooden porch steps. Then he was seeing himself and Mr. Lowell and Mr. Rutherford. He played with a yo-yo and with Beaches. Cooper gave the yo-yo to the boy in his dream who looked like himself. Beaches went up and down and rolled around to the rhythm of the boy's mouth yo-yo.

"Cool! You made him roll over! I wanna try!" Cooper heard his dream self say. He ran with Beaches to the front yard, and he trained the yo-yo again and again for the obedient dog. Then, Cooper tried to make Beaches do the same as the boy in the wheelchair had made him do.

The boy in the wheelchair, Cooper's lucid mind began to think. That wasn't him. He was not that boy. He was this boy, the one playing.

Dream Cooper dropped the yo-yo playfully and rolled around on the ground. Beaches joined him and licked him and pawed gently at his body. Cooper laughed heartily. He felt the chuckle shake his body from deep in his gut. He felt Beaches' paw against his shoulder. He felt the wetness of the dog's kisses on his arm. He felt the velvety softness of Beaches' fur. Cooper was feeling all of it and he was happy. He was living in the sensory moment of playing with his dog.

It was time to go in. He ran back up the steps with his dad and his dog while he smiled joyously.

"Some trick, Nicky. Some trick. I think you've earned some ice cream before bed."

Cooper's world grew dim. He lowered his head in confusion at the sound of the name. He felt a tingle of warmth blend with the cool brushing of an end of summer, dusk time breeze. He experienced an energizing sensation through to the very tips of his fingers and toes – his every nerve alive and dancing with the splendor of the atmosphere. He looked past the porch and saw, in one direction, Ashley walking toward the park and, in the other, Mr. Lowell pushing away a boy in a wheelchair.

Then, there was a warm tickle in his ear.

Cooper opened his eyes in a fog. It was just a dream. He looked at his open window, letting in the warm air that was still thick with the scents of desert shrubbery and red clay. The crickets were still chirping away in their evening glee.

Cooper heard, from down the hall, a joyful cry of "Yes!" from his mother in the kitchen. He sighed happily despite the fact that he was now scratching away the itch in his ear and, with it, the too real imaginings of the night.

As he nodded his head against the pillow, he closed his eyes once again and returned to a peaceful and dreamless sleep.

Chapter 8

A New Family For Christmas

The next few months were a whirlwind for Cooper. He didn't have the time to think about the dreams or visit Beaches and Nicholas as often as usual. He didn't do any of the typical things that kept him busy during the hours and days in which he wasn't schooling or doing physical therapy. Derek and April had decided on a December wedding with just a few months of prep time. Those preparations were constant and changing and they were all that the little family had time on which to concentrate.

Aunt May came by for longer hours these days, too. Cooper wasn't sure why. She would do his regular physical therapy – complete with the autos every single day (sigh). She was still his aunt and still his therapist, but she also seemed to be studying him more deeply these days, like their visits were just as important to her as a professional as they were for the sake of her nephew's health. She was watching and making notes and taking vitals more frequently. He had become, not just her family and her patient, but her case study.

Cooper didn't talk to his aunt about the dreams. He couldn't tell anybody. But secretly, he wondered if those were the very thing that were affecting his vitals and his health improvements. He knew how hard and heavily his heart throbbed when he slept and dreamt. He knew he felt tired in his muscles until he woke and, only then, did he not feel his heart or muscles at all anymore. Surely if he shared such imaginings, Aunt May wouldn't think him only disabled, she'd also think him deranged.

After his regular physical therapy, and sometimes during it, Mr. Lowell now stuck around, and Aunt May would be explaining things. Sometimes, she was even letting him help. It was strange to Cooper. He loved Mr. Lowell, but this new role of his—one that was so close to his physical handicaps—was an adjustment. As his educational mentor, Mr. Lowell had always focused on all of the things he could do, but learning about the physical therapies put the man right in the face of all of the things that Cooper could *not* do. It made Coop feel vulnerable, but it was an adjustment with Mr. Lowell becoming family he supposed.

Derek also came by earlier in the mornings and stayed later at night working on plans with his fiancé. Cooper's mom was still the one in charge of all of the other morning and end-of-night routines with her son; the ones that involved washing up and dressing or undressing, but Mr. Lowell was sometimes even there when Cooper was still in bed, which was an adjustment.

Although all of the transitions and the unusually hectic lifestyle that had settled upon the soon-to-be Ridge-Lowell household were hard, Cooper did enjoy the changes. It was nice to have a breakup to the usual routine. It had been difficult enough throughout his life to not be like others physically. When he also had to deal with the unique structure of his family compared to others, he used to be jealous of some of the simplest things, like watching a mom and dad have coffee together or sharing a car or talking about who was in charge of what chore or what errand needed doing.

Cooper never thought that those little things would be the ones he would most miss after he'd lost his dad. But those day-to-day activities were the things that took the very longest to get used to following his initial return home from the hospital. Even years later, on a rare sleep-in day, he would sometimes hear a news program on the television and coffee cups clanking on the counter and his brain would forget that it had happened, that the accident and his paralysis were real. In that time before waking up, when he wasn't yet fully conscious, he could picture his parents in the kitchen, and he would begin thinking about jumping out of bed to go get cereal. As soon as the thought became an intended action, of course, he was snapped back to reality.

With the impending nuptials, he was excited for his new family. His mom was still his mom. Derek would be his stepdad. He had a great aunt and uncle.

Life was good. The months since Derek had first proposed until the night before the wedding had flown buy in a happy flurry of "normal" familial interactions in which Cooper joyously basked.

Mr. Lowell didn't stay for dinner the night before the wedding. He left right after Cooper's Friday school studies. Aunt May and Uncle Harry joined them for the meal instead.

"So, tomorrow's the day, Coop," said Uncle Harry. "You excited?"

"Not as much as mom," he replied.

"You know," began April, "A lot is going to change around here."

"Duh," Cooper said. "You're not about to explain the birds and the bees and Derek moving in now, are you?" he joked to his mom.

Laughing, "That's not the only thing, though," said Aunt May. "There's something else we need to tell you."

Always sticking to humor over sentimentality, Cooper continued, "You're not getting married, again, too, I hope. I like Uncle Harry! Besides, that sister-wives and brother-husbands things is just creepy."

"Come on, Coop, be serious for just a sec," his mom said with a hand to his cheek.

"You know how Derek has been learning about your therapy?" May asked.

"Yes."

"Well, he's going to be taking over on those and doing a lot of that with you in addition to your schooling, alongside your mom, of course."

"Well, I guess that's okay. Will I still see you guys on pool days?" Cooper asked.

"I talked to one of the therapists about the pool, Cooper," said his uncle. "They've got you covered."

"Oh," Coop said, suddenly feeling like his perfect little extended family that he'd been building up in his head was not going to exist after all.

April chimed in, "And it's not like I don't know how to manage those tasks, too, honey. And you have the rehab center."

Cooper's confused expression was enough to prompt the bomb they were dropping.

"I got a new job, Coop," Aunt May said. "It's a huge opportunity. A lot of advancements are coming out of the facility I will be in, and my experiences and observations can make a real difference in people's lives. People like you."

"We'll be here through the wedding and for Christmas," Uncle Harry added.

"The job starts in the new year?" Cooper asked.

His aunt nodded.

"Not like I won't see you. You'll still visit."

"When we can. The thing is, your aunt's job isn't nearby," said Uncle Harry.

"Cooper, honey," said his mom.

That was her second "honey" in a single conversation. The added touch of his cheek, also a second time, carried with it the air of somebody about to tell his kid that his dog ran away.

"Aunt May and Uncle Harry will be moving to Washington state," she finished.

"It's a great job. We just couldn't turn it down. Physical therapy with a nonprofit community hospital," his uncle began describing quickly before his nephew could respond.

"I have two roles, actually," May said. "Sort of. I mean, I'm leading up a project that requires me to work closely with two unique groups of people. First, I'm providing the physical therapy and cross training routines for recreation department athletic teams. These are all incredible fully capable athletes. They even have a world championship Little League team"

"And the other group?" asked Cooper.

"Then I work with disabled athletes. That's kind of a mix. Some of them are people who were born with disabilities, some are new to their injuries and trying to make their ways back to full mobility. Others had injuries or accidents which caused a permanent loss of ability, but they're all athletes. Even some Special Olympians."

"You're a part of why she got this job, son," April smiled, proudly.

"Getting to work with you and watch your improvements has been instrumental in my understanding of how the human body works. I was able to bring a comprehensive approach to their program. And they are doing really innovative things. I may be able to make strides that others haven't ever considered before. I'm getting to work with the most incredible array of human physical ability and I'm gaining new understanding," his aunt went on giddily and passionately like he'd never seen her before.

"She may even make some of those strides for *you*," his uncle added proudly with an arm around his wife.

"Yes!" May exclaimed. "You should come visit, maybe as soon as spring once we've really gotten settled."

"That would give me plenty of time to fix up the house for you," said Uncle Harry. "It's a ranch. All one level, but I have to put up a ramp to the front porch, too. And there's snow on the ground up there, right now, so I can't get to working on that just yet."

Cooper was overwhelmed. He didn't say anything right away. He wasn't sure what he should say. It was a lot of information all at once. This was a lot to absorb in one sitting.

After a pause, "We were going to wait to tell you until after the wedding, but then we realized that there may be others there who already knew and we didn't want you to find out from one of them by accident," said his mom.

"We should have thought of it sooner," added Aunt May in unison with Uncle Harry's, "Sorry about that, Coop."

"No," Cooper said. "No, it's okay," he added more resolutely this time.

He made a choice to reflect his aunt's requisite positive attitude and he realized that it really was okay. Tomorrow, his family was changing in a lot of ways, but there were more good ways then bad. He always knew there could come a day when his mix-and-match community would normalize to the rest of society around him. Hell, he dreamed of it. His own dreams. He was about to have his mom and stepdad under one roof and his aunt and uncle were the type of extended family that one would visit . . . just like "normal" families. This was perfection.

They finished the rest of the dinner in anxious and excited conversations about the next day's events.

"See you tomorrow, sis'" Aunt May said as she grabbed their jackets to go. "You just call or text if you need ANYTHING at all, okay?"

"We've got you covered," added Coop's uncle with a kiss to April's cheek.

"Hey, Harry, before you go, could you put Cooper on the swing for me?" April asked.

"You'll be okay to get him back in afterward?" he asked.

"Oh sure. But I'm not going to turn away your help right now while you're here!" she said.

"I guess we're sitting outside, then?" Cooper asked.

His mom smiled, "It's gorgeous out. And you don't get to say 'No,' to the bride-to be. It's a rule."

"Okay, Bud, going for a ride," said Harry.

Cooper's uncle took down the head pieces and unstrapped his nephew from the chair before hoisting up his limp body to be carried to the porch.

A gel formed cushion with velcro seatbelt-like straps took up one side of an otherwise traditional porch swing. Uncle Harry was such a large, gnarly guy that it was a somewhat contrary act to see how gingerly he would set Cooper at the side of his mother. Then, the gruff uncle that Cooper had come to know and love came out again as he ruffled his nephew's hair ruggedly before setting on his way with Aunt May for the night.

"We love ya', guy!" he called back with a wave.

"Night," Aunt May added from the opened window of the car.

Cooper nodded upward and April waved lightly as they watched them drive off. It was already dark, and the night air was slightly chilly. April pulled a light blanket over her son and herself. The fireflies were flickering about in front of them and seemed to float upward into the sea of lights above.

"My goodness, look at that sky," said Cooper's mom dreamily. "A million stars visible tonight."

"Yeah," Cooper agreed as he turned his head to take in the nightscape above them.

"I like when we get to sit out here and just look at the sky. It always changes but is always reliable to be there, too."

"Ugh," Cooper huffed out a laugh at his mom. "You're such a sap, Mom. I know that things are changing. And I know that things will still be the same, too."

April laughed at herself. "Aww, come on. Give your mom some grace, will you? It's the eve of my wedding day. I'm too tired and excited for subtlety."

"I'll allow it," Coop smiled.

"It's been just you and I for a long time, Cooper. But it's never really been just us. I mean, other than when we're sleeping, we have a whole community."

"I know, Mom."

"And Derek loves you."

Cooper sighed deeply, not because he didn't accept the sentiment or because he didn't feel affection for the man who would become his stepdad. He just wasn't feeling the need for a deep conversation about it at the moment is all.

"I do miss your dad, Cooper. But I know he'd be smiling to see that we have somebody special to help take care of us and love us. You should know that. We'd talked about this scenario before."

"You had?" Coop was surprised.

"Well, not exactly this scenario. Not a scenario where our child was paralyzed and death was sudden," April took her son's hand in hers. He couldn't feel it, of course, but it was for her, not him.

"People don't really talk about those things," she continued. "But we did talk about what we would do or want if one of us ever lost the other. And I do know that, if the situation were reversed and I were up there and he were down here, I'd want him . . . and you . . . to be happy."

"Do you ever think about him?" Cooper asked.

When his mom turned back to him, she had un-fallen tears in her eyes. She took a deep breath, "All the time. I used to think about the accident and what could have been. I was angry for a while. Especially when I was first trying to manage it all."

April bit her lip and it's almost like Coop was in her mind with her on the day that they'd fallen. He could read the guilt on her face, not just for that day, but for the anger she had felt at his father for not being there to help. Then, she steeled her lips, sat up, blinked away her tears, and patted Cooper's hand in a more re-assuring way rather than in the security blanket man-ner in which she'd been holding it. She looked at her son and pushed his too-long bangs out of his eyes. He had at least gotten a haircut to clean up the sides and back, a sort of wedding gift to his mom.

"I think about the good times mostly now, though. I try to remember the very best moments and words and memories. I have a theory about those times, too. This is the perfect night to tell it," she smiled.

April looked out to their front yard and beyond. "You see all those fireflies flickering out there and all those bright stars up above? Well, I think that whenever a happy moment occurs and memories are created, the fireflies come along to carry them away. That's when they light up. They bring them to the sky, and they're stored in the stars. Then, those memories are flown back down at night while we sleep. The lights are dropped off then, the memories. They're given as dreams to children and to those who most need them."

Cooper's eyes got wide, and he could feel his breath in his throat hotter and quicker than usual. If he had felt his heart, surely it would have been racing.

"It's crazy and dreamy. Just a fairy tale," April added. "But on those nights when I didn't think I'd want to wake up the next morning, those nights that were just filled with fireflies, sometimes on those nights is when I would have just the most vivid dreams. And not just dreams of my own, but dreams of other people who weren't going through the same struggles as you and I. It was like I got to experience these little glimpses of normalcy while I slept."

"Maybe you should keep this theory to yourself," Cooper managed a joking tone to his mom.

Laughing, "Of course! If we let on that we know," she continued teasing, "they may not drop those dreams off to us!"

"Exactly," Cooper said, playing along with the tone, but beginning to form a theory of his own. "That must be why they only visit people when they are unconscious or just waking up or just falling asleep. Then, they can't get caught. They want to be anonymous dream givers."

"And we have to be ourselves when we're awake. Who wants to walk around stuck in the memory of somebody else's life just because the dream didn't have a chance to escape before waking up?" April surmised.

"Yeah," Cooper breathed out. "Who would want that?"

"Maybe some kid who lives in the freezing cold tundra gets the memory of one of us down here in the good old A.Z. and he's warmed all night long."

'Or maybe a boy who can't move dreams of playing ball?' Cooper wondered to himself but dared not say out loud. Instead, he and his mom sat quietly for a long time, and both watched the fireflies light up and take to the sky only to be replaced by new ones flickering and flitting about in front of them.

After some time with her mind still clearly on their discussion, "What sort of memories do you think our family has sent up there in our imaginary world?" April asked.

"I have a lot with you."

"Well, duh!" his mom joked, using an absolutely Cooper tone.

"I have one of Dad, too. I remember those boats we used to make. The model boats. I remember how much Ashley liked them."

Jumping in, "Oh, Ashley! I see. Is this really a memory of your dad or is it about your toddler-era fiancé?"

Cooper looked at his mom and couldn't prevent a huge smile from crossing his lips.

"You're getting married tomorrow to *your* fiancée," he said, moving the spotlight. "We are going to keep those fireflies busy carrying dreams all day long."

"We sure will, Bud. We sure will."

Chapter 9

Model Ships

The wedding went off without a hitch. A small ceremony in the yard with a buffet style cook-out. April and Derek ate and laughed and played yard games. Uncle Harry and Aunt May were dressed the nicest Cooper had ever seen.

His uncle wore khaki pants, and his shirt was even tucked in. Not that Cooper spent much time taking note of Uncle Harry's outfit.

Ashley was there with her family. She wore a bright yellow dress and she looked beautiful. When they played music, she even brought Cooper out to the hard floor they had rented, and she danced around with his chair. She made him positively dizzy, but Coop was sure that would have been the case even if Ashley hadn't been turning his chair and dancing around him.

The night went long, and the reception continued under twinkling white lights with propane heaters set around the festivities to keep it cozy. Ashley's family were some of the last to leave and she kissed Cooper's cheek.

He felt flush and this time he was sure it had everything to do with the girl.

After a long weekend getaway for Derek and April during which Aunt May and Uncle Harry stayed at the house to care for Cooper, Derek moved in. They became a real family. In no time at all, Christmas was upon the happy new unit of three that was added to by the extended family of Aunt May and Uncle Harry for one last joint holiday before they moved.

On Christmas Eve, they played Christmas music and watched *It's a Wonderful Life*. Aunt May danced with Harry around the room to *Jingle Bell Rock* while she did her best Brenda Lee impression. A couple glasses of April's spiced wine always turned her sister into a karaoke star and Uncle Harry was her biggest fan. Derek recited *'Twas the Night Before Christmas* with his own twists on some of the lines that nobody can ever recall. Close friends and dear medical team members they loved were called throughout the festivities and put on speaker phone. They even had a fake fire on the television.

Aunt May and Uncle Harry crashed in the living room, maybe by plan or maybe by necessity after just one more glass of wine. In the morning, the whole family cut and hanged paper snowflakes all around the room from different surfaces.

It was their unique family tradition to play Christmas music all day and, every time they heard the word "snow," the first person to grab a snowflake won the moment. Cooper had to make it to various spots around the room where they would mount the buzzers from all sorts of different games, and he would hit the buzzer with his head or nose. If he hit the buzzer before somebody else had claimed their snowflake, he was the moment's winner. At the end of the day, the person with the most snowflakes got the annual White Christmas Trophy, which was actually just an ice-skating trophy that April had found at a local thrift store. In reality, the words on it read, "Participant Award – Age 6 and Under Girls Skating." April, for her part, took the game very seriously and would turn into a parkour star throughout the day, leaping past people, over couches, and onto tables to be the first to a snowflake.

The gifts seemed to last all day as the family didn't open them all at once but spread them out as if they were a constantly reappearing afterthought to the real purpose of just being together. They all enjoyed the unwrapping done by each of the other people in the room. That was half the fun. Nicholas had stopped by to give Cooper a special joystick just like the one he'd been using at the friend's house. It was for a new baseball video game. He promised to come play every week until his real little league team started up in spring and he had to practice with them. His friend would age out after this year on the team, so it would be an important season.

Cooper, for his turn in the Christmas spirit, gave Nicholas a new heavyweight yo-yo that came with an app subscription to a trick-a-week tutorial program.

Aunt May and Uncle Harry gave Cooper a travel voucher to come visit them in Washington State. He was both excited and scared about that. He had only ever traveled for medical reasons. The idea of getting to go somewhere just for the joy of it was completely new to him. Cooper had given them a photo album he was able to digitally put together on his own and have ordered at the local pharmacy that did picture printing. His mom had taken all of the pictures, but he was able to select the ones he wanted to be included on the photo platform.

Cooper and Derek had picked out some truly unique treasures for April. Whenever she had gone to the thrift stores, there were things that she wanted for herself, personally. But since she was always thinking about resell value and whether or not they could be properly refurbished, she rarely purchased for herself. Separately they had each noted the items and had been gathering them for months. Derek also got her a dress that she changed into right away. She wore it all day long even while everyone else stayed in pajamas for the whole Christmas Day. In turn, Derek drank from the coffee mug his wife had gifted him to match her own mug. She and Cooper also gave him an assortment of other household matching items to go along with ones they already had as a way of making sure he felt as much a part of their home and family as he already was.

Cooper got new bedding featuring the colors of the Arizona Diamondbacks from his mom and he got a Bluetooth smart speaker that he could command with his voice. When it came to the gift from Derek, Cooper watched his mom open it, but he wasn't particularly excited. For the past couple of years during which Mr. Lowell . . . Derek . . . had been giving gifts to Coop, it was always something educational. Coop always used the gifts; they were typically something specialized and interesting. But nobody wants to think about school on Christmas day.

When April finished removing the paper from the gift, though, Cooper's jaw dropped.

"I hope it's okay," said Derek as he took the unwrapped gift from April and sat face to face with Cooper.

It was a model sailing ship, much like those that his father used to sail with him on the pond in the park.

"I'm not your dad, Coop, and I'll never try to replace him," he said. "But I'll be the best man I can for you and the best husband I can to your mom."

"It's like the one you and Dad kept looking at down at the hobby shop. Sails and old-fashioned looking," April added. "I think this was next on your list."

"I can't push these anymore," Cooper said and immediately regretted it.

He wasn't trying to put down the thoughtful gift. He was just somewhat shocked at it.

"They're remote controlled now," Derek began to show him excitedly, not at all offended by Cooper's initial reaction. "What do you think? Would you be willing to try it out with me?"

"I'd like that," Cooper said sincerely.

Then, something happened that he didn't expect. Derek kissed him on the forehead, just like he dreamed when he was Danny Mills, The Wonder Kid. He smiled back and the room suddenly felt uncomfortable. This was far more mush than his family's usual goofy Christmas. Cooper remoted backward and then away from the group. They watched him through the collective misty eyes they'd all gotten in the last few minutes as he made his way over to a wall and pushed a buzzer from an old game of Taboo.

"My snowflake!" Cooper called out to break the tension. "You all are so distracted that you didn't even notice that the song was *Let It Snow!*" he jibed as he hit the buzzer two more times while the song repeated its last time through the chorus.

Everybody laughed and the rest of the day went on with their jovial natures back intact. For the first time in his life, Cooper won the White Christmas trophy!

For dinner, Derek smoked a ham so tender that Cooper was able to enjoy a couple of finely diced pieces, along with a pea mash that Derek himself fed to him. That unexpected act was somehow not at all awkward. He also enjoyed squash and rice and hot cider and pumpkin pie filling, which is the best part of a pumpkin pie, after all.

When Aunt May and Uncle Harry left for the night, it was a long, tearful goodbye that seemed to never end. Every time they all hugged and kissed and said farewell, somebody would say something that triggered them to jump back into conversation and start all over again with talks about when they'd all see one another next and whether or not everybody and everything was taken care of. It was forty-five minutes of hard crying.

Cooper hated crying. His nose would run as heavily as his tears would fall and he'd feel like he had an awful cold. He got a hold of himself so that he wouldn't become so congested that his mom would have to hook him up to the ventilator that night. On the true, final goodbye, the rain started to fall, and it was even sadder to watch his aunt and uncle drive away in the middle of a rare Arizona storm.

Afterward, Cooper, his mom, and Derek came in and just sat quietly by the fake digital fire recapping the wonderful day. Cooper felt himself dozing, his head heavy with all the activity. Derek and his mom both tucked Cooper in for the evening. They put the new model ship on his dresser across the room. He would have Derek build a second shelf eventually, one to give this ship a place of honor alongside his favorite one from his dad. Tonight was so full of peaceful joy from the day that he didn't feel he needed the extra view just yet.

"I should close everything up," April said at Cooper's window. "All that rain out there is sure to keep you awake." April pulled down the shade and the entire thing accidentally fell. "Oh crap. I hate when it does that."

"It's okay, Mom," Cooper assured her.

"Well, let me close the curtains at least," she said as she started to take down the tiebacks and pull at the long drapes..

"No. Please don't. I like it opened," Coop said quietly.

"We'll fix it for you," Derek said. "Just not tonight," he smiled to Coop while putting a gentle guiding had to his wife's back.

The bat and yo-yo had fallen over when the shade came down and Cooper couldn't see them. He didn't say a word, but while his mom rolled up the shade and set it aside in his closet, Derek balanced the bat back up against the window ledge and placed the yo-yo on the nightstand next to the lamp, each in exactly the same positions as they had been in before. Cooper gave a knowing smile to his stepdad. Both his mom and Derek kissed him on the forehead and wished him a Merry Christmas night of dreams, then left the room.

Dreams, thought Cooper. *Who needs them on a night like tonight?* His mom had lain him propped up somewhat tonight. He was able to smile at the model ship from his father that rested on the shelf across from him. He sighed a happy, albeit slightly congested breath. In complete contentment, he drifted off to sleep.

Cooper looked down at his legs and feet. They were shorter than he was used to. He bent them up, then playfully hopped up onto them and began to run around a small pond. He could hear his own much younger laughter ringing in his ears.

"Wait up, Dad! He called. His voice sounded higher, smaller. "I wanna see! I wanna see!"

"Come on, little man, keep up. We have to do it from this side to catch the wind. Come on over!"

The man knelt down at one side of the park's small pond. A very tiny Coop ran right to his side and plopped down dramatically next to his dad. He looked into the water and saw his own reflection, that of a bitty five-year-old Cooper, staring back.

"Now what?" asked his child self.

"Now we launch it," said Cooper's dad. He was holding a small model sailing ship and he set it gently on the surface of the water at its edge. "Go ahead, you do it."

"How," asked the younger Ridge.

"Just a small push. You can do it. There's just enough wind here today that it should pick it up the rest of the way and we can collect it on the other side."

"What if it doesn't work?"

"It will. I promise," said Cooper's dad.

Cooper pushed the small ship lightly with his pudgy hand. The ship began a slow drift.

"It's barely moving," whined Cooper.

"You're right!" said his dad. "It needs a little help. Blow!"

Cooper and his dad flopped onto their bellies along the grass side of the park pond. The two laughed heartily while they puffed their cheeks out and blew repeatedly against the single sail of the ship.

"It's not enough, my boy! Bring in the motors!"

"What motors, Dad?"

"Splash! Go on, now! Splash!"

Cooper put his hands in the water and fluttered them about toward the stern of the little model. Caught up in the laughing he was sharing with his dad; he turned his splashes from the ship to his dad.

"Gotcha, Daddy!" he giggled as he splashed again and again at the man.

"Oh yeah?" the man joked back. "You know what I gotta do, then!" he exclaimed. With that, Mr.

Ridge scooped a handful of water toward his young son.

The water splashed through the air, and it hit Cooper in the face all at once cold and quick and wet. He flinched.

Cooper snapped awake in an instant feeling sure he had been doused in ice water. His whole body jerked in reaction. There was a warm tickle in his ear, and he lay motionless again.

It couldn't be. Did he really just move then? It had to be the dream. It must have felt real because it was a dream of his own past, a dream of a time that he had spent with his own dad. That had to be it. But, why then, were his toes out of the covers? Surely his mom and Derek had tucked them in. Or did they? He looked down at his exposed foot and panted heavily through his stuffy nose and dry mouth. If he could have felt his own heart, he was sure it must have been thumping wildly. His eyes teared up with exhilarated confusion.

He turned his head toward the window. The rain was still falling down. That's what it must have been.

Rain from the window splashed his face in his sleep. And his foot? Well, Derek wasn't used to the nighttime routine. He must not have tucked in Cooper's feet is all. Or maybe when the shade fell, it caught the bedding and pulled the quilt off of his toes. That had to be it.

Cooper methodically forced his breathing to slow, and he blinked away the moisture welling up in the bottom of his alert eyes. Finally, he let his lids heavily droop shut. The last sight Cooper saw before he slipped back into a dreamless sleep was that of a small firefly flying out the open crack of his bedroom window and up to the stars above.

Chapter 10

Cotton And Snow

The new year brought with it a terrible head cold that drained from Cooper's nose and throat straight back into his ears. The ache throbbed so deeply that Cooper cried in pain. A home doctor's visit led to some medicine and eardrops.

Derek gave Cooper a break from his lessons for a few days and let him watch movies instead, right from his bed. Cooper's mom, between guilty proclamations about allowing him to leave his window open on a rainy night, brought meal shakes and gave him even more welfare checks than his daily routine required. Mostly, Coop slept, but the ear infection just didn't seem to want to go away.

"I should never have left his window open that night; and with no shade, to boot!" Cooper's mom frustratedly ranted to Derek down the hall while Cooper listened.

"What difference could the shade have made, Babe?" he asked, trying to calm her down. "Stop blaming yourself."

"It's just that you know I can't sleep when he doesn't feel well," she went on.

"It's not your fault. Look, I'll even fix the shade. April, all kids get colds."

"Maybe. But most of those kids don't have to fear a ventilator when they get them, do they?" she continued, inconsolable.

Somehow staying calm, "The doctor said he doesn't need it right now. His oxygen numbers are great. You work so hard to keep the air pure around here, to keep this whole home clean and germ-free."

"I have to," she said. "He hates that ventilator. Feels like he's digressing. I'm so afraid of having to pull it out again, as much for his emotional well-being as for his physical health."

"Well, the antibiotics are helping the infection. Are the drops helping with the draining at all?" Derek asked.

"I think they're just draining right out of his ears, to be honest," April said. "He has to sleep propped up to help him breathe, so they just stream right back out, down his jaw line. They make more mess than they do healing. Maybe if they stayed in his ears a little longer, they'd actually help to make him better. "

"Not a big deal. Just put cotton in his ears at night. Then he can sleep propped up and the medicine won't drain out," he offered.

"Why didn't I think of that? It's so simple."

"Because Babe. You can't seem to get out of your own head when you get worried," he said.

Sighing, "I think that could work. It better. This is why I just hate for him to be sick. Do I make you crazy?" she asked.

"Yep," he said, and Cooper could hear the smile in his voice. "But I'm crazy for you, so it works."

That night, when Cooper was cleaned up for bed, his mom went to work to make him better. She fluffed up the pillows he'd been lying on for most of the last two days and she gave him his medicine and ear drops, then propped him up and put cotton into his ears to keep the liquid from draining. Now the medicine could do its job.

"I'm going to close your window, Bud," April said as she began to shut it tight.

"Don't, Mom," Cooper begged.

"But Coop—"

"No. Don't. It's not even rainy or cool. I like the air," he continued to plead.

Resignedly, "Alright. But you call me in if you get stuffy, okay?" she said with a worried expression.

"I will," Cooper promised.

"And I mean the very second, Coop, got it?" she pointed her finger in warning.

"Yes ma'am," Cooper half-laughed. "I'll tell my speaker to talk to yours."

"Is that sort of like your people will speak to mine for your generation?"

"Computer," Cooper said in a robotic voice, "Please tell April Lowell to go to bed and not to worry about her son."

"GO TO BED AND DO NOT WORRY FOR YOUR SON, APRIL LOWELL," the speaker down the hall was heard through Cooper's bedroom door. Coop and his mom cracked up and his laugh turned into a cough. April leaned him forward, made sure he was okay after wiping his mouth, and finally, she ruffled his hair, kissed his head one more time, and winked a goodnight before walking from his room.

"I'm leaving this door open, too, in case you want to just call out instead of asking your mechanical servant."

"No problem, Mom," he said. "Goodnight."

"Goodnight, My Cooper. I love you."

Cooper wasn't really tired since he'd slept so much lately. He mostly laid there thinking. He turned his head toward his open window and smiled drearily at his bat. Next, he looked at the yo-yo beside the small lamp on his nightstand. The light was left on a low setting while he was sick in case his mom or Derek needed to check on him in the night. He took in the sight of his two ships. The one from Derek still on his dresser since the holidays and the one from his dad on the shelf. He looked also at his new speaker, glowing blue in night. He had asked it to go off at 7:00 A.M., the same time as his mother's. It would play music from his top twenty listening playlist from the year before, at least until he got sick of those songs or learned to hate the tunes that were tasked with waking him up from his dreams. Nicholas had told him how he made the mistake of setting his wake-up alarm on his phone to the song from their favorite video game. Now, he couldn't stand the music in the game, anymore. Coop didn't want to make that same mistake. Mostly, he wanted to fall asleep before the alarms came. He was bored after days in his room, and he longed for the magical dreams.

It seemed hours had passed. Cooper's time finally grew dull enough that he began to yawn and wearily flutter his dry, dozy eyes open and shut. Then, he saw above him two little flickering lights. He looked toward them deliriously and was unsure if he was imagining things or if the miniscule sounds really were also floating about in the air of his room.

"Is this the right boy?" questioned the first light.

"That's him. He's almost ready." said a second.

The first asked, "He needs to be completely asleep?"

"No, just mostly.." the second light responded. "It's okay when he's just waking or just falling asleep. No coming or going when he's totally conscious. You'd have to wait for him to drift off again."
"Got it," the first tiny voice finished as one of the flickering lights flew out of the window.

Surely, Cooper's exhaustion and the medicines, or maybe the plugged ears, made him hear those high, buzzing whispers that weren't really there. Surely, the sounds of some passing car on the road outside or the rustling of plants outside had caused the noises. Surely, his imagination had put the words of such a strange conversation to the sounds. Surely. Because nothing else made any logical sense.

"I'm going to go check on him, Derek, and change the cotton in his ears," he heard his mom say from down the hall; her voice was crisp and clear, unlike the teeny sounds he had imagined just before.

"You know he's going to be fine, though, right?" Derek called after her comfortingly.

"I know. I know. But I'm checking anyway," April replied.

Cooper enjoyed listening to the light and playful love they each had in their voices with one another. He heard his mom's slippered feet sweeping down the hallway toward his room. The remaining small firefly—*was it just a firefly?*— flew toward the little lamp in his room and rested in its glow, almost completely camou-flaged by the light casted onto the nightstand. Cooper blinked away the sleep for a moment when his mom entered.

"Are you still up, Bud?" she asked. "Can't sleep?"

"I'm getting there," he said through a long, hol-low yawn."

"Just close your eyes and pretend and, before you know it, you'll be out. I just came to put in some fresh drops and change the cotton in your ears," she said as she pulled the small balls of fluff from his ears.

Cooper smiled tiredly at his mom and then al-lowed the night to take over, closing his heavy eyes even as April dripped new medicine into each of his ears. He heard his mom leave the room. Before she re-turned, his infected ear tickled lightly. He slit open his eyes groggily in a half-sleep and looked toward his lamp. He couldn't see the firefly at all. Although, he wasn't sure if it had ever been there to begin with.

While Cooper's mind floated into dreams, he allowed the sounds of his mother's returning to his room to melt into his nighttime imaginings. He felt her push fresh cotton into his ears, but he was already fast asleep. His eyes were rapidly moving in a dreamscape nothing like the room in which he actually lay.

"Good hit, Son," said the man across from the small barn where Cooper stood with a bat. A white square was drawn with chalk on the red wooden planks behind him.

"I think it's going to be a great season, Dad," Cooper said. "Matt's got an awesome new curve and he's still got a wicked fastball. I think we're going to take the championship for the fifth straight year."

"You have to make the team, first," said the man. "I don't want you getting all full of yourself and thinking that, just because you're last year's MVP, you'll have an automatic in. You have to try out just like the rest of the players."

"That's why we're practicing, right? Almost two months to tryouts."

"That gives me plenty of time to try to show my son he's still got a thing or two to learn from his ole man!" the elder joked as he threw the ball hard into the white square behind Cooper. "STRIKE ONE!" he called.

"No fair. You caught me off guard," said Cooper.

"Then put your guard up, son!"

Taking a batting stance, "All right, then! Try me!"

"The man threw another perfect pitch toward his son.

Cooper swung hard at the ball and felt the impact of it against the bat buzz down the Louisville slugger and vibrate in his wrists.

"Who's got something to learn now," the younger man smack-talked his dad. "That one is long gone!"

"That's it!" said the older man in a faux-angry tone. "Catch!" he called as he threw the solid white ball at Cooper's head.

"Hey!" Coop shouted, suddenly afraid as he quickly duked away from the impact.

It turned out to be only snow. Cooper's heart settled back down out of his throat as the snowball splattered against the side of the barn.

"Like I would actually throw a ball at my kid's head!" his dad said.

"That was a cheap shot, ole man Mills!"

"Well, that's what I've got left so long as you keep getting better and I just keep getting older, young Danny Mills!" he chided back.

Cooper refused to open his eyes even though he was just called Danny Mills. He could feel himself fighting to stay asleep. He could feel the dream struggling to get away. He squinted his eyes tightly shut, willing the fantasy to stay.

No, he thought. *I want the dream. Ignore the name. Don't wake up. Don't wake up!*

The two men tossed some bare-handed snowballs at one another. One struck Cooper in the shoulder and split open, spraying snow into his ear.

"Hey!" he reached up to brush off his ear.

Cooper snapped awake and simultaneously the cold sprayed ear from his dream became the infected one from his real life as it filled with a warm tickle. Cooper looked at the window and saw a firefly making a quick and crooked escape as though it had been trapped in a jar from which there was no exit, and it finally was able to flee. But that firefly wasn't the only one with an escape plan.

Cooper looked down at his hand – the one with which, in the dream, he had brushed off his snow-dusted ear. A cotton ball lay in that hand. Cooper had pulled out. He was sure of it, and, for the first time, he understood everything.

Chapter 11

Letting The Dreams Go By

"How'd you sleep, Bud?" Cooper's mom said to him in the morning after they'd both awaken to their smart speaker alarms.

"Fine."

"What's this?" she asked when she spotted the cotton in her son's hand.

"It fell out," he lied.

There was no need to talk to his mom about what he knew or how the cotton came to be in his hand. Soon, he hoped, it wouldn't matter.

"Oh. I'm sorry about that, son. I must not have tucked it into there tightly last night. I was a little tired, too. How do your ears feel today?"

"I think the trick worked. Cotton is a miracle cure, Mom," he smiled wryly at her with a groggy voice; he had barely slept after his discovery, so his words were still lazy.

"You still seem a bit tired," she said. "Were you up again after I checked in on you?" she wondered aloud as she brushed his forehead with the back of her hand and adjusted his covers and pillows much as a nurse would do for a hospital patient.

"A little," he fibbed for a second time.

"Well, I'll tell Derek to hold off one more day before he starts up with your lessons again. I'll bring you in a nice breakfast drink and I'll wrap your throat in a warm towel,"

"Thanks," Coop said.

"You want me to wheel the tv screen in here again to stream a couple of movies?"

"Nah," he said.

"Too bad. Ashley said she might visit," April said.

"Oh!" Cooper lit up. "I guess I could watch a movie," he smiled.

April pursed her lips, but Cooper could tell that she was holding back from sharing a teasing comment, "I'll be sure to bring a nice chair in for her to sit in. And we'll maybe clean you up a bit before she gets here. Getting a little ripe in this space."

After a sniff to the air and the inevitable sour facial expression that followed, "Maybe a good idea," Cooper admitted.

Ashley came over late morning. It was a virtual day at school, and she had finished her work already. The two streamed a rom-com that Cooper never would have chosen. But, while he didn't enjoy watching the movie, he did enjoy watching Ashley . . . as she watched the movie. She laughed and cooed throughout the flick and, when it was over, they talked about friends and activities that had started up in the second semester of her junior year. Cooper hadn't met many of the people she talked about, but he'd heard her share their names often enough that he was able to keep them straight in his head.

"Anyway," she finished breathlessly, "that's when Meaghan said she refused to take French anymore so long as Jamie kept at it. So, she switched to Mandarin. And that's the class Blake is in, and Blake is like way better for her, anyway. Blake is the new guy I was telling you about."

Cooper's mind was elsewhere. He smiled thinking about the cotton that had been in his hand, the soft feeling of it against his skin in the fraction of a second before he woke. Then, he imagined the softness of Ashley's skin, her cheek under his fingertips. He imagined the feel of her lips on his. And then he looked at those lips.

"What?" Ashley asked with a strange expression.

Coop didn't realize he had been staring.

"Huh?"

"Do I have something in my teeth?" she gritted her mouth in front of his face close enough that he could smell her perfume.

"No," he laughed as she sat back down. "No, I was just . . . um . . . looking," he said with a smile.

"Oh," Ashley said. She put her head down and grinned bashfully. "Well, I should probably get going. Your mom told me you'd been sick and couldn't really hang for long."

Cooper didn't try to stop her. He had used all his boldness by his admission that he was looking at her.

Nicholas visited later in the day, but Cooper struggled with the new joystick while still being a bit congested, so they mostly just caught up and told one another about their holidays. Nicholas had already started to train for baseball, too. He was attending a skills clinic prior to tryouts and spring training. He felt good about how much was learning. Cooper flashed back to hitting his dad's pitch in the dream as Danny Mills and he dazed out again.

"What?" Nicholas asked.

"I'm sorry," Coop said. "I keep getting distracted today."

"It's cool. I gotta get home, anyway," said Coop's friend. "I'll visit again after you're feeling better to let you get in some practice time on that new stick."

"Thanks, man. I'll take the fighting chance."

Cooper continued in his happily dazed state the rest of the day, constantly thinking about the dream he'd had, the realization that followed, the plan he imagined, and the hope for the future. In between his friend's visits, Derek listened to a sports podcast with Coop. He promised to bring Cooper to a game again this year and he wouldn't even have to keep stats. April had brought both lunch and dinner straight to the room and joked about being his maid. Aunt May and Uncle Harry called to check on their nephew and to talk about the hectic realities of their move. Tomorrow the routine of life would begin again. None of those in Cooper's world realized that the routine would have, as an engine under it, a new dream, not just in Cooper's sleep, but also in his heart. Even while he faced the most mundane of routines, he had a kinetic energy building up and getting ready to burst out.

With peaceful optimism, through every boring act, the sixteen-year-old was secretly waiting for something else . . . for something more.

Regarding his continuing education, Cooper now had the added benefit of being able to relax and joke a little more with Derek . . . err, *Mr. Lowell* . . . they decided that he was still his teaching title during the day, but Coop wasn't sure it would actually last. They both seemed a bit confused with the teacher/stepdad combo, but they would adjust. The strict standards of his tutor remained the same even while the lines be-tween home and school got blurry.

Cooper had to take psychology this semester and he asked Derek to bring materials to let him study lucid dreaming.

"Lucid dreaming? What's got you interested in that?" Derek asked.

"It was in one of the movies I saw when I was sick," Coop lied for a third time. He was getting good at that. "It's where you can be aware in your dreams and help control it. Some people even interact with their dreams."

"I know what it is. It's just a really specific sub-ject is all."

"But it can count for my psychology class, right?"

"I'll check. Probably not the whole credit," his tutor said. "But I'm sure it fits into one of the units. Happy that you're excited to learn something other than sports stats, though. I encourage learning."

Mr. Lowell had grown used to doing the physical therapy exercises and the autos with Cooper. Or was that Derek that was doing those? Coop didn't know. Yeah. This Mr. Lowell stuff was going to have to go! Derek was different than either Aunt May or his mom.

Aunt May was always all business. Cooper's mom was always kind and gentle. Derek tried to be both, but he wasn't really comfortable being either which made his leadership during therapy as awkward as the swapping of names. He sometimes seemed nervous and other times a bit too commanding. Each time grew a bit easier, though. Cooper enjoyed being the one who had to instruct the instructor whenever Mr. Lowell forgot how to set an auto routine or perform a particular stretch. He was good with taking vitals, though. It seemed something as solid as numbers was right in his wheelhouse. One day, his new stepdad commented that all of Cooper's stats were looking good, so they must be doing well together.

Derek was surprised to see Cooper going above and beyond in psychology, really digging into any materials the tutor could find for him on the topic of lucid dreaming in addition to any of his assigned studies. The tutor didn't know that Cooper was waiting for something else . . . for something more.

Cooper finally was sleeping well through the night again for the first time since he'd been sick. He no longer had cotton put into his ears at night and his dreams returned.

That first night of sleep, Cooper dreamed of going to the high school with a whole staff of teachers, somebody different for every subject. He set up his very own locker with pictures of all of his favorite baseball players. And with a picture of Ashley.

It felt real.

He could feel the cold metal of the locker and hear the clicks of his new combination lock.

It was his own dream. It's not the dream he wanted. He was secretly waiting for something else . . . something more.

Cooper let it pass peacefully away from a warmed and tickled ear and his sleep became dreamless again. He remained aware of his surroundings even as he continued to slumber.

Nicholas came over once a week to practice yo-yo or play games. Sometimes the two boys would watch a movie. One week, he brought Beaches along and both practiced training the dog with their yo-yos. Nicholas went through an entire pocketful of treats. Then Nicholas left to take the dog on a run through the neighborhood.

That night, Cooper dreamed he was taking a run with Beaches through the neighborhood. He waved to every neighbor he passed and most waved back in turn. He saw Ashley sitting on her front porch.

It felt real.

He could feel his feet bounding along the sidewalk. He could hear the panting of his pet beside him.

It's not the dream he wanted. He was waiting for something else . . . something more.

Cooper let the imagining pass peacefully away from a warm and tickled ear and his sleep became dreamless again. He remained aware of his surroundings even as he continued to slumber.

Cooper had even more one-on-one time with his mom since Derek became part of the family. Because Derek was always around, his mom didn't have to go out to be with him. So, her time could be spent on occasional mother-son date days with Coop.

One day, she woke him early and cleaned him up. April put Cooper into his chair, and they went on a walk through the neighborhood for the annual community garage sale. She often found some of her best treasures for her business here, and Cooper loved to help her spot them.

The ice cream truck stopped across the way from one of the sales and Cooper watched as Ashley and the girl he'd since learned was Meaghan got ice cream sandwiches from the man in the truck.

Ashley waved to Cooper. He felt his cheeks get hot.

That night, Cooper dreamed he was walking through his neighborhood for the annual garage sale with Meaghan. The ice cream truck stopped and the two of them got ice cream sandwiches. He looked across the street and saw himself, the teen in the wheelchair, and he waved. Meaghan giggled.

"I can't help it," he heard himself say. "We get along. And he's kind of hot."

This dream interested him. Was he Ashley? Was she talking about him? His own heart started to race. Or was that Ashley's? If it was Ashley at all. He wanted to stay here, tasting the ice cream, laughing with the friend, and discovering if Ashley could possibly look at him the way he looked at her.

It's not the dream he wanted. He was waiting for something else . . . something more.

It was harder with this dream, but Cooper let it pass peacefully away from a warmed and tickled ear and his sleep became dreamless again. He remained aware of his surroundings even as he continued to slumber.

It was March; a perfect Saturday morning. The sun was shining in the crisp, blue sky and the scarce breezes were light and cool. The Ridge-Lowell family of three got up nice and early and had breakfast together in the kitchen. Then, it was time for a guys' day out, according to Derek.

"We'll be home about five, April," he said to his wife before kissing her goodbye and loading Cooper and himself into the handicapped van they owned to go for a drive.

"Where we going?" Cooper asked.

"We're going out for lunch and to some stores. First, though, I'm taking you to watch Nicholas's tryouts. Mr. Rutherford said his son could really use the support. He's pretty nervous. I thought you'd enjoy watching them, anyway.

"Definitely," Coop said sincerely.

Cooper had been back to the park where he was injured many times since the day of the accident. It had taken some time initially, but once he got through the first couple of visits, beginning about two years after the crash, he was okay with it. He even had gone on "walks" with Ashley on the paved trail that surrounded the whole park a couple of times. He would remote while she walked beside him and spoke dreamily about earning a solo in the school concert or getting a speaking part in the latest community theatre show. He had far more positive memories in this place than negative ones. So, he couldn't quite figure out why he was rushed by the flood of trauma as the park came into view on this day.

Cooper was eight years old again. He was right there with the sound of his dad's laughter, the way his eyes twinkled, the playfulness that made his dad feel more like a friend than a father when they were at the park. The summer sun was bright that day. Ashley pretended to be in their game of catch but really, she just played in the grass by Cooper's feet distracting him from time to time. His dad had just thrown the ball and was calling to him to catch it as he simultaneously ran toward Cooper. It was their last throw of the day, and they were headed out. Cooper's eyes were on the ball and nothing more. He didn't hear the people scream as the speeding car jumped the curb. He didn't hear his dad shout or notice Ashley fleeing. He felt his dad's arms around him before the ball reached him and he heard a loud crash and then, he couldn't move.

Ashley was hiding her face. Cooper was paralyzed. His dad had taken the full impact of the truck and died on the spot.

"We're here," Derek said. "You okay?" he asked looking at Cooper.

"I'm good. I'm good," Coop said.

He would be good. He had a way out. That had to be why he thought of the terrible day now. Because he would finally be able to leave that day behind.

The two men had a great time doing all of the things that Derek had promised.

Cooper had the sense that Derek, or maybe Nicholas, had primed the other players about how to treat him. Many of the guys had stopped by him on the side of the bleachers to say hello and almost none of them seemed to notice the fact that he was in a wheelchair. It was a little too on the nose, really. Nonetheless, it was sweet in its own way.

"Good of you to come by, son," Hank Rutherford said when he came over, and he ruffled Cooper's hair, but it wasn't welcome from the man who did it condescendingly rather than comfortingly

"Dad, you know he's actually older than me by a few months," Nicholas said. "Maybe stop talking to him like he's Beaches."

Cooper tried not to smile. He never realized his friend even noticed. Mr. Rutherford looked embarrassed.

"Sorry, Cooper," he managed, which is more than Coop ever expected, so he was grateful.

"We're good," Coop said sincerely.

Cooper and Derek ate at a new restaurant called *Soup's On* which served nothing but soups, breads, and salads. Cooper had a huge selection of brothy meals from which to choose. Then, the men walked through a sports store and looked at all sorts of things.

In another store, they tried to find a good video game, but couldn't put their hands on one that would work well for Cooper. Nicholas must have worked incredibly hard to discover those he'd found over the years. Cooper would have to find a way to thank him for the special attention. At the day's end, just before returning home, they got ice cream.

On the drive home, Derek and Cooper discussed all of the great and not-so great players they had witnessed that day at tryouts. Thankfully, both agreed that Nicholas was good enough to make the team. They weren't sure when the results would be posted, but Nicholas deserved it after all the practice he'd put in.

That night, Cooper was tucked into his bed as exhausted as he imagined any almost-seventeen-year-old could possibly feel. With much difficulty, he forced himself to remain aware of his surroundings, even as he drifted into slumber.

There was a dream he wanted, and he was waiting for something else . . . something more.

Chapter 12

The One He Was Waiting For

Cooper never felt himself fall asleep. He never felt the tickle in his ear. It was almost as though he had floated out into the batting cage on that practice field, much like the misty fog that was settled upon it now. He took a deep breath of the wet, early spring air. He looked down at himself in the baseball attire, a Washington Wonderboys scrub uniform. He looked at his own hands and feet and he knew himself.

This was the one he'd been waiting for.

Cooper was sure of it.

He wanted to revel in the moment of the dream, but he had to focus on lucidity. He had to hold onto his senses; he would need them soon enough. His heart began to beat hard with anticipation. Would his plan even work or was he as crazy as he was crippled for even considering it. He knew what his cue would be. The name. Wait for the name. The name always came before the dream ended, regardless of which name or which dream. Cooper forced himself to remain calm in his sleep to keep the dream. He must not wake yet. He was waiting for something else . . . something more.

Only after the name came would he will his entire self to make the impossible happen, if it could.

Don't think about it, he told himself. *Be in the dream. Be in the dream and wait for the cue.*

It was pretty cool out today, and overcast, too. Nicer temperatures didn't usually arrive in his western Washington state hometown until about May. Cooper found it strange that he knew these sorts of things, but that's always how it worked when he was in the dreams. He knew what the characters in his dreams knew. So, today, he knew that the wind was coming straight off the Pacific which was not a good thing this time of year.

The Saturday morning air was damp and thick, and it was hard to keep warm, even with his jacket snapped all the way up over his practice uniform. He pulled his cap down tight over his forehead, shading his eyes against the cold and blinking away the wind-incited tears that felt like they would freeze on his face. He sniffled lightly and shrugged his shoulders, stretching his head and neck in a back and forth rolling motion. He yawned widely. Cooper stood up jumpingly, then paced about so he could warm up his muscles at least as much as his nerves.

His turn would come, but right now it was time to watch the pitching and none other than his best pal Matt was on the mound. He wished his dad would get back soon to watch the event. He had dropped Coop off to run and grab some coffee for himself and hot chocolate for some of the players. Cooper wanted to hold onto a hot cup more than drink it, he thought as he balled up his hands into fists and stuffed them into his jacket pockets. He just couldn't seem to shake the morning shivers. Others on the bench were huddled up, but Cooper knew he had to get psyched for the try-out and not let the hour of the day or the weather of it keep him down.

"Not bad, Hill, not bad at all!" said an approving coach with a deep slow nod to the pitcher. "You've been working on that curve ball, haven't you?"

"Yes, Sir!" Matt grinned back proudly.

"But how's that fastball faring since you've been giving all this new attention to the curve?" he prompted the player.

"Hope that catcher's mitt's got extra padding," Coop's best friend confidently smirked.

Cooper didn't think this pitcher looked anything like the Matt who had been shifting back and forth on his feet in the championship game last season. He smiled at his friend out there some fifty-four feet away and he shook his head laughingly at his buddy's bravado.

Coach looked to his Wonder Kid and chuckled to, as if to say, *'Well, he's your friend!'*

For a moment, Coop thought his cue might be coming and he nearly awoke, but the coach just dropped his head and turned back toward the mound. Cooper breathed slowly and deeply, and he allowed his eyelids to remain thick and heavy.

"Alright, Matt, let's see it!" said the man in charge.

"That was it!" the pitcher grinned.

"Very funny, Hill. You're fast, but you ain't that good!"

"Just joshing with you, Coach!" Matt laughed.

He was in great spirits. Cooper actually felt sorry for the poor couple of guys who came to try out for pitcher. They might be a good backup guy, but they would never be the go-to player so long as his pal was still around. Although, there was nothing shotty about being a relief pitcher on a championship team, either. That is, as long as the guy didn't mind sitting out five of the six innings in each game.

Coop's best friend barreled in pitch after pitch. Only one ball the entire time; all the rest were spot on, and fast! All of the batters who tried out with Matt on the mound begged for another try with somebody else throwing a few for them.

Finally, Coach just broke down and told Matt, "You made the team, already, Hill."

The coach waved one of the other pitchers in. The young man appeared to be disappointed at the prospect of likely trying out only for the relief pitcher position. Matt made his way back into the dugout.

"Glad you're on my team," Cooper said while bumping Matt's fist.

"Oh, you mean *my* team!" his buddy returned with a smack to Cooper's back, a smack he felt with every nerve. "You still gotta make it!" he joked.

Once again, Cooper almost woke up with the anticipation of a name that didn't come. His ear grew warm for a moment, but it didn't tickle. He calmed his heart. The dream, which had grown blurry for the shortest of moments, returned with full clarity. *Keep your senses*, thought Cooper. *Keep the dream but keep your senses.*

The fog had burned off or at least risen above the field for the most part as the Saturday carried on and a hazy, spring sunshine flooded over the anxious auditioners holed up in the cage like cattle waiting to be driven. This year's cattle made a longer list than ever before. Therein was the complication of having a great sports reputation. Everybody wanted to be a part of the team. From the youngest eligible to the oldest, not to mention those who tried to sneak in by pretending they were younger or older than they honestly were, there were players lined up and signed up to show their best. It was clear that some had barely even held a bat or ball before stepping up to the plate or out to the field or onto the mound. This made the early started morning drag to nearly noon before Coach had narrowed down the field to serious contenders.

Mind you, there is obviously something very good about a championship reputation, too. The very best came out to join the Washington Wonderboys. This year's competition amongst the potential players was fierce and the team would be great for it! Keeping warm would certainly no longer be a problem once Cooper began moving around against and alongside his possible teammates.

Coop didn't mind so much that there were a few other good hitters in the mix. It was the fielders who had him worried. He had been hoping to move up to shortstop this year and some of the other final year boys had such great speed out there that he wasn't sure he'd be able to hold his own. His dad, who had returned at some point to cheer on his son and his son's best friend, assured Cooper that it wouldn't be a problem for The Wonder Kid!

Cooper's number was called for speed trials, and he hung in with the best of the players running the bases. He opted not to throw any pitches. Even if he could keep up with his friend, which he couldn't, he would never want to challenge Matt's position on the team. When it was his turn to bat, he was quietly grateful that he was pitched to by a boy who would probably make a good relief pitcher but was nowhere near as tough as his friend. He got off a fly to an uncovered position and a grounder that led to a double.

"You're doing great, son," said Cooper's dad with a strong, squeezing pat on the shoulder when he'd returned from the batting portion of the try-out. "Just one thing left. You'll do just fine," he reassured his son.

His dad's eyes gleamed with joy. Cooper waited for something more . . . for a name. But it still didn't come. He squinted tighttly and forced his heavy breathing to slow in order to calm his heart. His cue would come soon enough.

The two waited patiently through some of the best and worst playing they had ever seen on display for the Wonderboys' coach. Even some of those who had made it to the final cuts based on great hitting or throwing just didn't have what it took to make it work in choreography with the rest of the team on full plays. Matt stuck around to support his friend long after he was done with his own work in the try-out.

Finally, it was Cooper's turn to practice fielding. He went deep first. Then, he had to throw from each base. Finally, he was near the baseline as shortstop.

Ball after ball was sent his way high, low, on the ground, to either side, and every which way possible. Time and again, the ball didn't get past Cooper. He dirtied that uniform through and through and sacrificed his body for the stitched sphere the same as he would have done for a real game. His dad in the foreground was a blur of fists in the air, jumping about and, once, hugging his pal Matt after Cooper had stretched his long body out particularly far to catch a ball just as it was about to bounce in the dirt.

When all was said and done, Cooper had only missed one ball thrust his way. The next person closest had missed four. It would have been a pure injustice for Cooper not to have made the team. They would be hearing the results, next. Cooper forced his breathing once again to slow. He couldn't believe the dream, the memory, lasted this long. Cooper knew there was no way his cue wouldn't come now. Coach was going to read off the roster and that would bring the name for certain; that would bring the cue. That would be his chance to prove to himself that this was real.

He saw the blurriness of the dream as his heart began to beat hard in his chest. He barely clung on to the drowsy state necessary to keep the nightscape rolling, but it was enough. He needed to be alert and asleep at the same time.

"Alright boys, great job today," began Coach. "Now, when I call your name, come on up next to me and you will be my starters. The rest of you that still remain here are on the team, but you're bench for now. That could change as the season goes on and you practice. So, don't go getting soft on me or walking off. Hard work will pay off on the Washington Wonderboys I reward effort. That's a promise."

Cooper breathed deeply in his bed . . . and in his dream.

"Matt Hill, Pitcher!" said the coach.

Next, Coach read off the name of the catcher, 1st base, 2nd base, 3rd base . . .

"And for shortstop, we have a new starter this year," he began.

Cooper took a long, slow, calming breath.

"Danny Mills, come on over!" he called to Cooper.

That was it! In an instant flash, a second of time at most, squeezing his eyes shut as tightly as possible, Cooper willed every bit of his dream self to come to life as he slapped both of his hands up fast and hard against the sides of his head before the different name had time to snap him from his imaginings.

"WAKE UP!" he shouted boldly out to himself and then he forced his eyes wide open.

His ears were hot and tingling, but there was no tickle. Cooper panted hard; his hands still tight against his ears; so tight that they throbbed in a vacuum of humming. There was a muffled ringing too. He held his eyes open as largely as possible in the dim night glow of his room. His gaze raced about, taking in all that was around him and the waking world was coming into focus. He saw the model ship across from his bed and he felt his own heart beating rapidly in his chest. He saw the window cracked open and he felt the breeze upon his body. He saw the nightlight and could even feel the hairs on his arms that rose in the yellow beams of its light.

With his hands on his head, he dared not move another millimeter. Cooper continued to visually scan all that was around him, willing himself to believe that he was in his room and no longer in his dream.

"Cooper!" called April in a midnight panic stumbling down the hallway. "Cooper, what is it?" she shouted as she threw back the door, entered his room and rolled the knob-like light switch near the entrance to turn on the overhead light in his room to maximum brightness. She looked at her son and gasped a stifled scream. "Oh my God," she finally managed weakly.

Cooper turned his eyes toward his mother who still stood frozen in the doorway, her own hands held against her dropped jaw and mouth, a look of combined panic and exhilaration upon her face.

"DEREK!" she screamed. "DEREK GET OVER HERE!"

Coop kept his hands clapped tightly against the sides of his head and breathily, shakily, trembled out the question, "Mom . . . Mom, am I awake?"

His eyes watered and he lay still except for his wildly shifting gaze still taking in the reality of his setting.

As the panicked and clunkier steps of Derek came down the hallway, April wordlessly shook her head for a moment, seeming unable to form words.

Finally, as she stared wide-open-mouthed at her son, she stuttered a reply of, "I don't know. I don't know if I am."

"What's going on?" Derek asked as he charged the room and joined April at her side in equal shock.

"I'm awake," said Cooper again and again. "I'm awake. I'm awake."

In an almost trance-like state, Cooper did the unthinkable in front of his mom and stepdad. Keeping his hands on his ears, he slowly lifted his body away from the pillows. The action was so slow that it looked almost magical, supernatural, like when a magician makes a lying woman rise above the stage. Then, Cooper turned his legs and sat on the edge of his bed looking at April and Derek.

"I'm awake," he said again as unwilling tears began to stream out of his eyes and he blinked them out repeatedly while they continuously rained down his cheekbones.

In his head, Cooper played back the voices he'd heard over his bed months ago:

"He needs to be completely asleep?"

"No, just mostly. It's okay when he's just waking or just falling asleep. No coming or going when he's totally conscious. You'd have to wait for him to drift off again."

Got it, Cooper thought to himself as a reassurance.

"I'm awake," he said through rapid breaths and a fluttering heartbeat.

His tone was strong, as though he were giving himself an order of some kind. He stared glossy-eyed at his mom and stepdad. Then, he swallowed hard, hoping against hope that he would be right as he closed his eyes, lips trembling in a panicked cry. Very slowly, deliberately, and cautiously, Cooper lowered his shaking hands from the sides of his head. The blood in his arms was buzzing. Then, he reopened his eyes like slow-rising suns to an unknown day and he resumed calming breaths, still methodically scanning his surroundings.

"No tickle," he said with a broken voice through his throat lumped with emotion. He felt the thickness in his neck heavily within him as he continued in his call of, "I'm awake. I'm awake."

Cooper bawled openly as he sat on the edge of a bed.

Finally, and silently—except for an exhale that seemed to have been on hold for a decade—April dropped her own hands from her face and drifted floatingly to her son. She kneeled before him on the floor in front of the bed and, after putting her hands on his cheeks with a transparent need to feel that he was real, she stared into his moist eyes. Then, she sobbingly wrapped her arms around him, weeping in his lap as though she were the child who could not speak in this overwhelming moment.

Derek then clumsily made his way over to them, too and plopped beside Cooper on the bed. He tearfully, and tightly slid an arm around each of them.

"Yes, you're awake," Derek said. "We're all awake, but it feels like a dream, Coop. It feels like a dream."

The family of three, in a private time when the world at last seemed fixed, was broken down into wails of grateful disbelief.

Chapter 13

Being Awake

The wordless weeping shared by Cooper, April, and Derek went on for some unmeasured time. It was still dark outside, but none of them cared about the hour. Cooper's teardrops finally slowed to a trickle and eventually stopped flowing entirely. He looked at his clock. It was 12:28 A.M. *Time of birth*, he thought.

Gently, Coop took Derek's arm down from around his shoulders and he pushed his hands deliberately against his mom's shoulders, lifting her carefully off of his lap. Every move he made gave him confidence to try more.

He unattached himself from the tubes he'd seen his mother unhook before, careful to protect himself from infections; no colostomy bag or vital sign monitors for him. April gasped at first, but with a look from Cooper, she reached over and clicked a button to turn off the new tones that had erupted when he'd disconnected, and she turned off his mattress. The only sounds associated with Cooper's body, the only monitoring of it, was to come from Cooper himself as he felt and experienced each movement, each gesture, and each breath.

April and Derek still couldn't find any words. They just watched in disbelief as Cooper moved his hands this way or that, like he was putting on a performance. He raised both hands up high and looked at them as though they couldn't possibly belong to him. He pulled them down into a bicep muscle pose.

Cooper pushed his mom and Derek to either side of him and he looked at his legs, sizing them up, running his fingers over his thighs and bending double over himself to feel his knees and shins and calves and feet. He touched each toe scientifically and wiggled it with glee. Cooper was like a toddler picking at each digit curiously as if they were colorful keys on a toy. He sat back up, one vertebra at a time, while tracing his fingers up his legs until his hands were in his lap. He squeezed each leg.

Cooper took a deep inhalation. Biting his lip and looking down at his feet, he rotated first his right ankle, and then his left. His eyes were squinting, and his brow was furrowed as though concentrating hard to make it happen, He pointed and flexed each foot. Cooper's lips spread open int oa crooked, batty smile. His eyes shifted around trickily as if he was still taking in the scene around him, still convincing himself of this new reality. He was hungry for more experience.

He looked at Derek and his mom as if to say, *'Should I?'*

He bent one knee, and then the other . . . very slowly. Cooper then planted his feet, which had been hovering and inch over the floor as he hung his legs off the side of the bed, onto the hardwood planks beneath him.

"Don't push yourself," Derek managed through bated breath, while April was still too overcome with crying to say anything.

"I'm fine," Cooper whispered in focused concentration.

He pushed the palms of his hands into his mattress on either side of himself and pursed his lips. He raised his body away from the bed and into a standing position.

"Cooper . . . how . . . but—" April began.

Cooper jumped on his legs, causing a tiny jump from his mom, too, and he landed hard and flat footed. He shifted his weight back and forth on his feet, the way he'd seen Matt Hill do on the pitcher's mound in the Wonder Kid dream. He bent both legs down so that he was squatting, and then he stood back up. Cooper spun around in the air to face his folks and his mom let out a frightened yelp.

As for Coop, there were no more tears. He grinned broadly down at them. His heart was beating quickly, and he pushed his hands against his chest to feel it thumping within him. He absorbed every sensation. Cooper was so tuned into his own body that he could almost feel his blood flowing . . . buzzing through his veins and arteries. Suddenly, a light breeze brushed his face and Cooper inhaled the clean night air that had come in through the open bedroom window. The minigust left the baseball-decorated curtains billowing in the air. He expanded his lungs to their full capacity, pushing out his stomach and felt the cool breath fill him up like a human balloon. Cooper looked huge and he laughed at himself. He looked past April and Derek in a trancelike state toward the window.

"Oh," Cooper cocked his head to one side. "That's different," he said as he looked down. His leg had gotten warm and wet. "Wait!" he shouted as he stopped from continuing to wet himself. "I know this feeling. I remember this feeling. I gotta go."

"You what?" his mom cried.

"Ha! I gotta go!" he laughed.

With that, he turned his back to them and started walking from the room. The steps began small as he crossed his room to the hallway. April and Derek both rose to their feet very quickly. April wanted to put a hand on her son, but her husband stopped her, allowing them to be close, but not to interfere. Cooper held his hands out to the sides with his fingers spread out as if he needed his whole body to walk. He began to take larger strides and, eventually, halfway down the hall, his hands fell to his sides and swung somewhat normally while he tried to relax his shoulders. By the end of the hallway, he was practically marching.

"Go where, Cooper?" a panicked April said. "What is going on?"

The bathroom door closed at the end of the hallway. Derek and Cooper's mom tried not to listen but couldn't help overhearing a trickling sound, then a pause followed by a flush and water running in the sink. Next came the metal clunk stop of the faucet being turned off and the squeak of the hanging towel ring. After the awkward moment, Cooper flung the bathroom door open and stood in the doorway with his hands proudly planted on his hips. Silhouetted against the yellow light of the room behind him, Cooper looked like the profile of a hero.

"I did it!" he said as he punched his fists into the air. "Terribly, mind you. The floor is a mess!" he laughed, and his mom and stepdad joined in.

Cooper turned from the bathroom to explore other parts of the house. His pace had picked up to an easy jog across the house. He went down the stairs, with his mother objecting the entire time, but he bounded back up in no time.

"Mom!" he shouted to her as he passed by at the top of the stairs again, "Your workshop looks great!"

He continued to explore at a rapid pace all the way to the front door, which he thrust open with eight-plus years of pent-up strength. Every door he threw open seemed to make him stand a little prouder and a little stronger. The front door slammed against the wall behind it just like the bathroom door before had done against the bathroom wall and the door to the basement after that.

"Cooper?" asked Derek as he entered the living room with his wife right behind. "Maybe let's slow down. You're making your mother nervous. You're making us all nervous. We need to call the doctor."

"Why?" he said.

"Because you're...." April began before realizing she didn't have an answer; you called doctors when somebody was hurt, not miraculously healed.

Cooper looked out the front door and didn't turn around. Instead, he stepped out onto the porch and began to casually stroll all the way down his wheelchair ramp and the driveway until he reached the sidewalk. He beamed back at the two once more with a touch of mischief in his eyes. Then, he turned away to look down the street and broke into an all-out sprint.

"COOPER!" April screamed after him in a frantic voice. "Cooper, no! It's the middle of the night! Come back!"

Cooper ran on, though. He was tired of listening. Tired of going only where others led him.

"You get the van," Derek said with a kiss to April's cheek as he took off after Cooper.

Meanwhile, Cooper ran as fully as a body possibly could. Each step was like a leap, and he swung his arms big and high. And he was fast! Derek couldn't catch him. He called after him and some of the neighborhood lights started popping on in windows they passed. Cooper kept on, pounding the pavement in quick cadence as he felt the night air rush against his face and whistle past his ears. His lungs were on fire, a feeling he greatly enjoyed. He made it to the end of the block and ran right into the street. Nobody was out at this hour. He crossed without even pausing to look for traffic and he ran on. One house had a lawn and a nighttime watering sprinkler. He ran right through it and circled back to do it again, then one more time. He saw the headlights of the van coming toward him and Derek had nearly caught up, so he crossed to the other side of the street and ran full out in the other direction back toward his house.

Derek hopped into the van.

"COOP!" April scolded.

The van turned around in a driveway and Derek got in. The two caught up to Cooper just as he made it to the house right next to their own. Derek and April pulled into the driveway and Cooper plopped down breathlessly at last on the ground of his own front yard. His throat grew tight with thick breaths and a throbbing pulse. He spread his arms and legs as though he were frozen halfway through making a snow angel. He wanted to make his body as big as possible. He stared up at the sky and panted away his own vigorous run.

April ran to Cooper's side.

"Don't you EVER do that again," she shouted. "Never ever ever!" she screamed. "I was worried sick!"

"Are you insane?" Derek joined in. "And are you okay?"

"Never better, Cooper gleamed. "Never better," he said jumping to his feet again.

"Don't you go running off again," April started in, and she squared off against her son who now towered over her.

"I'm not!" Cooper said.

He threw his arms around the necks of both Derek and his mom, and he squeezed them tightly with all the power he could muster. Finally, some of the tension in them softened.

"Come lay down," he offered. "The ground is nice," Cooper led them like a child to a sandcastle.

"But—" April objected.

Cooper had already lain down. Derek plopped down on his butt beside his stepson.

"We need to call the doctor," she pled.

"It can wait, Babe," said Derek. "How about let's just take in the miracle first?"

April stared at them incredulously, breathing deep to calm herself. Lights in the neighborhood started to go back out, probably under the assumption that it was just some teenagers playing.

"I'm calling as soon as we go back in though," she said.

"Okay," Cooper shrugged. "For now, sit." He patted the ground next to him.

They stayed outside the whole night. They listened to the night air sweep through the dessert bushes like maracas, a serenade to their midnight miracle. There was no sleep for any of them despite the aged hour. They lay in the yard until the dark sky melted into purples, then pinks, and finally a majestic, fiery pool of oranges and yellows. A hopeful sun was rising, and birds were singing, and Cooper simply concentrated on absorbing every sensation of the dawn into every inch of his being.

Chapter 14

Living The Dream

After what seemed like hundreds of phone calls to Aungt May and Uncle Harry, other relatives, friends, neighbors and everybody whoever knew or even heard of Cooper, April, or Derek, there was a solid month of media frenzy. News programs, online papers, podcasts, and medical magazines all wanted to put their angle on the miracle boy. Sports organizations, schools, and rehabilitation groups wanted to hear what he had to say. Every local feel-good group, regardless of what they were about, was asking for Cooper Ridge, the miracle boy . . . Cooper Ridge, The Wonder Kid . . . to be present at some function or other.

There were doctor's appointments, of course – and tests. His body had been adapted over the course of years to accept and release nutrients in manners that had to now be returned to normal functions. He looked forward to doctors not being a part of his routines. Plus, there were more appointments and more tests just to figure out what had happened. Most spoke a whole lot of theory and possibility but didn't have actual answers

"It makes absolutely no sense, Mr. and Mrs. Lowell," one finally honest doctor admitted while looking bewildered. "He should not be moving at all. Even if he could, it still doesn't figure that he should know how to do the things he can do or that his body was not atrophied to the point that they were impossible. Many of the activities you describe are learned actions, not instincts. One simply does not lie still for eight and a half years only to wake up running like a track star," the man continued to shake his head. "I'm absolutely perplexed. Clearly, he is strong and healthy and downright athletic but why?" he shut Cooper's now bursting medical folder as he stated the rhetorical question. "I don't know. Medicine doesn't always have the answers and I sure as hell don't. If I were in your shoes, I'd simply be grateful for the blessings I'd been given and I'd appreciate every moment I had."

It was those "moments" for which Cooper lived. Not only was every single new feeling one in which Cooper indulged—from sweating to itching to standing in a shower and letting the water run over himself—but every single action was one he would use as an excuse to push his new bodily workings to their limits. Every morning, Cooper awoke to his alarm blaring, and he would hop out of the bed dancingly and plant his two feet against the cool, hard floor and wiggle his toes beneath him. He would do loud, exaggerated stretches and he'd jump up and down in his bedroom as if he were a monkey on a big, room-sized trampoline. Throughout the day up until the now very late hours he stayed up, he continued that big way of living and moving with every act he did.

Derek returned home from some errands one day with a package for Cooper, "Got something for you!" he said with a casual grin as he tossed the box in front of Cooper.

Cooper tore into it like a starved man at a buffet, "My own glove!" he called excitedly as he jumped up.

"Yeah, I was thinking—" began Derek.

"Thanks, Derek!" Cooper cut him off with a half pat to his stepdad's back. "I'm going to show Nicholas," he called back as he ran out of the room with his new glove and without noticing that Derek was holding a ball.

He used the glove, not just for baseball, but also as an oven mitt, and a hat, and a shade over his face when he lay outside. Anything he could adapt to doing with that glove was done in such a manner.

That night, as with every night since the miracle, April and Derek tucked Cooper into bed, with his window cracked open. It was the one concession he made, allowing them to still have a nighttime routine. They said it would go away in time, but they daily checked vitals and some movements the rehab doctors wanted to have regularly recorded. He also would wear a smart watch that tracked his quality of sleep. Sleep is the one area over which his medical teams agreed he was not healthy. Not a lot of deep sleep and abnormal levels of REM sleep plagued the young man.

Once his mom and stepdad left his room, Cooper would arise, go get cotton from the bathroom, and tiptoe back to his bedroom. He'd close his door behind him, shut his window, and ball the cotton up tightly into his ears, pushing it deep inside so that there was no chance of it coming loose.

Coop missed the variety and complexity of the dreams he used to have. After the miracle, the dream he had each night was torture. There was no longer a different story; only the same one. Once he would finally slip into an uneasy sleep, he'd relive the tense team try-out for the Washington Wonderboys. He slept with unwilling anticipation for the name that was bound to come. When at last the coach called out, "Danny Mills," Cooper tossed over through the fogginess and the aching blows against his warmed ears. The dream couldn't escape, though. It would then grow clear again and loop back for a replay. Throughout the night, Cooper would drift in and out of sleep trying to hold onto both the dream and his sanity at the same time. He was caught in limbo between the waking world and that of his imagined realities.

Every day, Cooper ran down the neighborhood street at a full sprint. When he passed Ashley's place, he would call out to her, showing off. She sometimes called after him, but he was unstoppable. Cooper didn't understand why she didn't talk to him anymore. He could finally be a regular guy for her.

Coop also sometimes would run right past Derek taking a walk in the neighborhood. The man carried a baseball around like a wallet these days. It hung out in Derek's back pocket like a lump, and he'd sigh disappointedly as Cooper passed him by like an invisible presence.

When Cooper fell down on his runs—not because of the inability of his legs, but because he paid no attention to obstacles and sometimes tripped—he would relish the stinging pains brought by the sidewalk or road. He even smiled through the cool cleansings that dissipated the burn in the scrape.

"Your body may work differently, now," his mom said to him while putting antibiotic gel on the latest cut he couldn't reach, "but you still only have one of them, just like the rest of us. You need to start being more careful."

"Thanks, Mom," Coop said with a kiss to her cheek before taking off, again, as if April had said nothing at all.

Had he looked back he would have seen her face fall into her hands. He would have seen Derek come to her side and pull the baseball out of his pocket. He would have seen the two of them hold onto one another, not in celebration of Cooper's recovery, but in sadness over missing him.

He didn't see any of that, though. He was almost to the park before that scene had unfolded.

That night, once more after the nighttime routine, once more after his window was shut, once more after the cotton was stuffed into his ears, once more as the familiar dream returned, Cooper was caught in limbo between the waking world and that of his imagined realities.

In the afternoon, after local schools had let out for the day, Cooper would run to meet Nicholas at the park, and he'd watch his friend's team play. Cooper hadn't been able to try out for the team, but because his miraculous recovery had made him into somewhat of a local hero, he was allowed a uniform of his own. He was the bat boy, and he was the ambassador for their whole season. He didn't know why they called him an ambassador, but he got to toss out every opening pitch for them. One week, he even tossed out each game's opening pitch. He ran between the four municipal fields making the rounds to get each game started, all while a news camera followed him. It made a national good news story. Sometimes he would get to run the bases to open or close important games, too, and he basked in the echo of his name being called in the stands by his community.

After the games were done each Saturday, while Derek sat with April in the bleachers and a hopelessly optimistic look on his face, an unnoticing Cooper would shout, "I'm going over to Nicholas's house, now! See you guys later!"

The two would smile but looked drained.

"It's probably going to be like this for the first year of first activities," Coop never heard Derek reassure his wife. "It will pass. He'll come back," he said.

And, of course, that night, as with every night, after his window was shut, once more after the cotton was stuffed into his ears, once more as the familiar dream returned, Cooper was caught in limbo between the waking world and that of his imagined realities.

In the evening when families had retired to their own homes, Derek and April would attempt to enjoy a meal around the table with Cooper. Both would ask about his day and his plans with the team.

"You know," Derek began at one such meal, "Nobody is playing on the field this weekend after the games. And also, the fields won't be raked and chalked until Sunday. I asked the groundskeeper. That means all of Saturday night is free."

"I have an idea," Cooper said excitedly.

"Yes?" responded an equally expectant Derek.

"Mom! How about I can take some of these ribs down to Nicholas? I love this sauce!" he exclaimed, completely ignoring Derek.

Food was another new love of Cooper's.

"I suppose," she said, somewhat shocked. "But maybe first you want to finish."

Cooper was gathering up most of what was left on the table and putting it onto a sheet of aluminum foil before heading for the door.

"See you in time for bed," he called back absently as the door shut behind him.

It was April's turn to console. When Cooper had been a quadriplegic, he was keen on listening. But he missed all of their words lately.

Derek threw his napkin on the table, his optimism finally broken, "Dammit!" he said.

"Like you said, it's all just new to him," she said while stroking her husband's arm.

"We're last on his list," he said. "We aren't even in this new Cooper's life."

Cooper was home in time for bed as he promised. After his window was shut, once more after the cotton was stuffed into his ears, once more as the familiar dream returned, he was caught in limbo between the waking world and that of his imagined realities.

Spring melted into summer and summer burned its color into Cooper's flesh, now tanned and freckled with healthful youth just as Danny Mills had been in the Wonder Kid dream. Each of Cooper's days was spent fully awake, frolicking in the pleasures of the world. Each of his nights was spent with the window shut and cotton in his ears, fighting a dream that would constantly return and replay – a dream that was trying to escape, the dream that kept Cooper caught in limbo between the waking world and that of his imagined realities.

Chapter 15

Washington And The Wonderboys

fter another nearly sleepless night, Cooper was awoken, not by his alarm, but by his mom's cell phone.

"Hey sis!" April answered. "I've got you on speaker because I'm cooking. Can you hear me okay?"

"Yeah. You're fine," Aunt May's voice rung out in the air. "How have things been? I feel like it's been ages since we spoke."

"It's different. I mean, of course, it's a gift. It's a miracle. It's still so hard to believe. Some days I wake up and get halfway down the hall to his bedroom to start the morning routine before I remember that I don't even have it, anymore. But time is flying so fast, too."

"What do you mean?" April's sister asked.

"I feel like Derek and I haven't even gotten to take part in this new life of his, she sighed heavily.

After a pause during which Cooper could hear his mom chopping something or other for breakfast, "Remember when you had that cast on in the seventh grade?" his aunt asked.

"Fell off Mindy Parker's skateboard and landed at the bottom of the gazebo stairs. That hurt like hell."

"That's the time. But as we get older, it's the cast you remember and the break that led to it," May went on. "You don't really remember what happened when you got it off. At least not past the ice cream dad got us afterward. But you were in the pool almost every day swimming."

"I loved swimming," April said joyfully.

"But you were the only one of us who did," said Cooper's Aunt. "Not the rest of us. You were just kind of barely around in our lives for, I don't know, it seemed like longer than the time than you were in the cast. Coop's been in his version of a cast for more than eight years. He has a lot of swimming to do, sis'!"

"Or, in his case, running, I suppose," April said back.

Cooper heard his mom scrape off a cutting board into a pan followed by a sizzling sound. She must be making omelets.

"I didn't even ask why you called, May. I know we've been dealing with this unexpected positive, but you've had that negative situation. How's that boy doing?" Cooper heard April ask.

The tone of the conversation changed, and his mom must have moved to the other side of the kitchen. He couldn't hear Aunt May, anymore. He just picked up on his mom's occasional concerned, *"Oh,"* or a genuine, *"I'm so sorry, sis',"* and ultimately, *"I just really wish there was something I could do."*

April came back into hearing range with the phone at that time and he heard his aunt say, "Actually, there is. I think it would be really good for Cooper to come visit, to bring a little inspiration to the young man. He's got that travel voucher we got him for Christmas. We would really love to have him. What do you think?"

"Oh, May, that's a great idea! I think it might be wonderful for everybody involved. And, May, you and Harry deserve to see Coop. You won't believe it. Have the tissues ready."

There was talk between the two women of dates and times and, as the call came to a close before the inevitable loves yous and goodbyes, his mom and aunt had his travels all planned out. He crawled out of bed, pretending to be just waking up, and went to the kitchen.

"Good morning, Sleepyhead!" April said as she put a plate before him and started to fill it up with a half of the omelet from the pan. She sat next to him at the counter.

"Where's Derek this morning?"

"Getting coffee. We're out," April grumbled and grinned at the same time. "SOMEbody keeps drinking it!" she added with a playful shove to Cooper.

"That's good stuff," Cooper said. "I never knew."

"It's fine. I'm just giving you a hard time," she said as she took a bite of her food. "So, I spoke to your aunt this morning, Bud," she prompted.

"Yeah?"

"Well, do you remember how she works in two areas, with people who have disabilities and with top athletes?"

"I remember," he said.

"Her worlds kind of, well, they collided."

"What do you mean?"

April began picking at the eggs on her plate, a maternal concern taking over her words, "They have this little league team there, The Washington Wonderboys."

Her words seemed to echo endlessly in his raw, aching eardrums. He tried not to react, but he felt his cheeks grow hot.

"What about them," he managed quietly.

"Well, apparently," she paused with a sigh. "I don't want this to bring you down.

"I'm fine mom. Just tell me."

"One of the boys on the team became paralyzed this year. Nobody knows why. He was the MVP last year . . . a very healthy, athletic young man, same age as you. While you've been living this wonder of recoveries, that young boy has become a quadriplegic and isn't able to move," April finished with a look to her son.

Cooper stared at his mom with glossy eyes. His mind was racing. *It has to be a coincidence,* he thought. *It couldn't be the Washington Wonderboys from his dream.*

"I knew it would be hard for you to hear about such a thing," his mom added with a touch to his arm.

Suddenly, he didn't want his food, anymore. Cooper felt a tightness in his throat and his heart quickened.

"I know you're still getting used to your own new life, but Aunt May and I were hoping that you might be able to go visit her. She really needs to be around something good now, Coop," said his mom.

Cooper had a sense of fear and panic. His aunt's worlds were colliding, but so were his, the waking world and that of his imagined realities.

"We also thought that maybe you could meet this boy," She added. "He doesn't have what you had – not the same quality of life and maybe not even the length of life. It takes more than just good will to make it. It takes a lot of things that maybe you might have taken for granted and they didn't come cheap, son. I can't explain it all, but we were really lucky."

"Lucky? I was lucky?" Cooper said incredulously.

Indignant, "Yes. You were. You'll see for yourself when you go out there."

"What? I'm going? But you didn't even ask me!" he whined.

"Why are you so upset? I thought you'd understand, Cooper. And you'll get to visit your aunt and uncle, too. Why on earth would this not be something you would want to do?

"I just don't want to," he shouted as he threw his fork down onto the table.

"Cooper," April said sternly as she stood with her plate and went to the sink. "You're going. I can't believe, after everything you have been given, you can't so much as share your time," she went on angrily scrubbing her dish and also the one she had snatched from her son and scraped into the garbage disposal. "Although I guess I shouldn't be surprised. You haven't shared any time with Derek or I, either. Believe me, Son, it's the least you can do for your aunt. But who is she to you anyway, besides the person who helped keep you ALIVE for eight years?" April was now shouting.

Cooper stared back at her, still glazed over. His mother had never scolded him before that he could remember. Ever. He was in shock.

"Coop, I don't even know who you are these days," she went on. "You disappoint me."

"It's just that I—" Cooper started stumbling, but he couldn't really come up with a good reason as to why he should not go see Aunt May and Uncle Harry, much less an acceptable excuse to get out of meeting the boy he hoped he didn't already know, the boy whose name he refused to ask because he was too afraid to hear it.

Just as Derek walked into the door, Cooper stood up frustrated, and stomped out of the room.

"What did I miss?" Derek asked his wife. She stepped into his arms crying and Cooper could still hear her as he slammed the front door and started running.

Two weeks after the argument, but with he and his mom still barely speaking, Cooper found himself, his new glove, and a bag of cotton balls on an airplane. He was headed north with a suitcase full of clothes beneath him in the belly of the plane. He slept the whole trip up with his baseball glove as a pillow and cotton in his ears, of course.

"It helps keep my ears from popping," he told the flight attendant who looked at him strangely when he stuffed the balled-up fluff deep into his ear canals; lying had become second nature in his new life.

When Cooper got off the plane, Aunt May and Uncle Harry were waiting excitedly outside of security to greet him. He spotted them searching the crowd of exiting passengers to see their nephew's face. They scanned right past him twice. Finally, when he made eye contact with his uncle and mouthed "Hi!" his uncle's jaw dropped. Uncle Harry squeezed Aunt May's shoulder and pointed. Immediately, May's hands went to her mouth, and she shook her head in disbelief. Cooper could see the wells of tears sparkling in her warm eyes.

"Oh, my heavens, COOPER!" she gushed as he joined their outstretched arms. "You're so tall," she said laughingly as she looked up at him.

"You look great, guy!" said his uncle, his cheeks appled up with an infinite, ear-to-ear smile.

Cooper felt in many ways that he was reliving his first movements again all day long. Aunt May and Uncle Harry kept staring and had painted on grins that never seemed to wear out. Occasionally, his aunt would break into uncontrollable fits of giggles – something Cooper had never witnessed from her in the past. His uncle, big teddy bear that he was, kept wrapping Cooper up in big, unexpected, strong, tight, man squeezes. The three spent that first day catching up, getting Cooper set up in their guest room, and going out to eat. Uncle Harry laughed heartily when his nephew ordered a steak at the restaurant. The server must have thought them crazy.

In the days following his arrival, Cooper began to think that he'd escape having to discover the inevitable reality of why he was here; meeting the Washington Wonderboys and the boy who was paralyzed. The night before Cooper's departure for home, though, Uncle Harry popped in on Coop in the guest room.

"Got something for you, guy!" he grinned while he tossed a baseball cap at Cooper. The teen turned it around and saw the logo that was an unmistakable match with the one he'd seen in his dreams. It was a

Washington Wonderboys cap, with Cooper's own name added above the logo.

"Why don't you grab that glove you're always toting around and come with me?" said his uncle.

"I'll need my glove?"

"Well, it's a baseball field we're going to! Can't think of a better place for it," Uncle Harry said.

The drive to the practice field was filled with the stats and histories that Uncle Harry had learned about the local championship team.

"They're still playing?" Cooper asked.

"Well, they won't make the playoffs this year. Mathematically impossible. But they've still got a couple of local games left."

When the two arrived, the team was out on the diamond in the midst of a practice game against themselves. Cooper looked out to the mound and inhaled an involuntary gasp. It was Matt Hill.

"He's really good," Cooper noted after watching Matt wing in a few pitches.

The ball seemed to whiz by faster than he could remember . . . if he could remember. Was it his memory? It was all so confusing.

"They're all good," said Uncle Harry. "They're all great, actually. But they lost the game in their hearts, this year. They just weren't in it."

"Harry!" called an older man coming to the fence where Cooper stood with his uncle. It was the coach, another face Coop immediately recognized.

In his head, the worlds he was never certain were connected, began to collide.

"Glad you could make it down!" exclaimed the man. "This must be the boy, then?"

"Yep, my nephew, Cooper Ridge. Miracle. He's *our* Wonder Kid." Both Cooper and the coach seemed to flinch simultaneously at the statement. "Coop, you can call this man Coach," finished Uncle Harry.

"Hey ... *Coach*," he stuttered awkwardly.

"What are you doing on that side? You brought your glove, right? Come on over. Play a bit with us!" he responded cheerfully. "You can use this!" he added with a broad grin while he brandished a baseball bearing the stamped symbol of the Little League World Championship Game. "It's yours after today if you want it. Last one I've got. Was never sure what I'd do with it until your uncle told us you'd be coming to visit."

Cooper looked to his uncle for permission, almost hoping that it wouldn't come, but he nodded with proud approval. Cooper donned his glove and went around the fence to join the Washington Wonderboys. Part of him kept waiting for the world around him to grow blurry. It never did. As unbelievable as it seemed, this was real.

"Jump in at shortstop, why don't you?" directed Coach.

"Yes, sir," Cooper said.

The boys on the team all had stopped to watch Cooper walk across their field. He could hear their whispers. He could feel their eyes on his legs, watching him walk. As he passed Matt, his pulse began to race.

"Hey," called the pitcher to him, "You that kid who couldn't move last year?" he asked.

"That's me," Cooper said. "I was paralyzed." The words sounded stupid and obvious to him.

"Cool," said Hill. "I mean, not cool that you were paralyzed, but cool now," he corrected himself.

"Thanks," said Coop, feeling like a fraud.

"You should come by after practice," Matt offered.

"I guess," Cooper was caught off guard by the invitation. "I have to make sure it's okay with my aunt and uncle."

"You do that. Now, get out there," said Matt with a nod toward the empty shortstop position.

Cooper remembered a different Matt from his dream of the season's tryouts. He remembered a boy who was confident and fun and playful. This young man came across as strong and determined and—Cooper hated the thought—a little bit bitter, too.

They played for a couple of hours. In the outfield, Cooper didn't let a ball by. There seemed to be in him some inherent knowledge of the skills necessary to working that position. Even though the baseball was constantly punching against the leather of his glove, though, Cooper felt like he didn't belong there. He wasn't enjoying the game.

When it was his turn to bat, Coop swung and missed against Matt's first two pitches. Then, on the third, he circled that bat down hard, strong, and straight, ending with a resounding smack against the wood. The ball flew farther and farther out, still too high to be caught by the Wonderboys in deep field. Finally, a slow, arcing descent culminated in the ringing bell-like clangs of the ball against the metal bleachers outside of the fence. It was a homerun.

Cooper ran the bases to the cheers of the Washington Wonderboys and experienced, for a moment, complete contentment. It may have only been a scrimmage, but he had given his all and done his best. Then, as he felt Matt's eyes burning holes into his running legs and the feeling of elation faded. Once more, he was steeled in the fact that he did not belong there.

When all was said and done, Cooper gathered his glove and met his proud looking uncle outside the fence. Much to his dismay, Uncle Harry had already met Mr. and Mrs. Hill and agreed to let Cooper visit them for dinner. The ride to the Hill house was tense. Cooper didn't know what to say to any of these people and Matt had plenty to ask of Cooper.

"So, what did you do the day before you started moving again?" he questioned.

"Nothing really. I went out with my stepdad," Cooper said.

"What did you eat?"

"I don't remember. I think I had some soup. The rest was nothing different than usual."

"With a feeding tube?"

"I didn't have a feeding tube or breathing tubes. I have a special thing – kind of like a pacemaker, but for my diaphragm instead of my heart. It makes, or it made me breathe more regularly."

"What else did you have? Stuff to help you out? Did you have a nurse or—"

"Matt," Mrs. Hill finally chimed in. "Give the young man a rest."

Matt said he was sorry for the third degree, but he still looked at Cooper in a way that Coop could only interpret as resentful. His own mouth turned upward in a meek attempt and friendliness before he looked outside the car window for an awkward and silent remainder of their trip.

Finally, they were pulling into the family drive. It was a farm. Something seemed familiar. The car stopped in front of a red barn. On the side of the barn, a batter's box had been chalked. It was partly erased from rain and wind, but the pasty, white residue that remained was clear enough to make out as something that had obviously been drawn in the same place time and again over the course of many months or even years.

"Hey," said Cooper getting out of the car. "Isn't this house . . . I mean," he stopped himself. "This is where *you* live?"

"Yeah," said Matt.

"*Just* you guys?" Cooper asked.

"Now. My friend and his dad used to rent the barn. The whole upper floor of it is converted to living quarters. Little kitchen and bathroom. The whole works."

"The lived in the barn?"

"Not always," Matt said casually. "My dad and his dad were friends their whole lives. When my friend's mom got real sick with cancer, they spent everything they had trying to make her better. But she died. They had nothing and we had that space. So, they came here."

"Where are they now?" Cooper questioned with genuine concern in his voice.

Matt sized him up for a minute before answering. "Danny is in a facility."

Cooper had his confirmation. He hated the sound of the name that he had once yearned to hear and that now tortured him every night while he slept.

"His dad, Mr. Mills, has to work a lot to afford the place that takes care of my friend, and we told him he could stay here, but he didn't want to be any trouble," Matt continued. "So, he's got some tiny little place in town just for himself. It's closer to Danny and he can walk to see him. His car isn't too reliable."

"Sorry," said Cooper.

"Well," interrupted Matt's dad with a change of subject. "Let's get in and feed you boys after you worked so hard out there on the field."

Dinner was uncomfortable for Cooper. Although the Hill family was certainly hospitable and the conversation was civil, he couldn't help but feel like he was on display the whole time. When his aunt arrived to bring him back to the house, he was relieved.

"Oh wait, May!' interjected Mrs. Hill as Cooper and his aunt were headed out. "I have some things for Danny. You'll be seeing him tomorrow, right?"

"Yes. I'm bringing Cooper," she responded, and Cooper did a double take because his aunt hadn't told him yet about the impending visit and he had still been hoping that it had been forgotten in the itinerary.

"Well, come back in for just a quick second. I have to bag up the clothes."

Cooper and his aunt returned to the tense household once more and followed Mrs. Hill to a back bedroom where she had clothing lain out that had clearly just been washed and folded.

"I know it's not much," she began as she stuffed the clothes into a bag, the jeans with beige stitching, the striped polo t-shirt and there, he swallowed, were the signature white leather tennis shoes. "It's all I could get from the church in his size. Tell him that we promise to bring some more . . . you know . . . *modern* clothes just as soon as we get paid. I know these aren't exactly on trend."

"Oh honey," said Aunt May, "You know that boy! He is just grateful for everything your family sends. It doesn't matter to him how it looks!"

Cooper felt shame as he noticed the moisture glistening off the fake-smiling eyes of Mrs. Hill and she said, "I'm so sorry. I can't believe I still get like this." She fanned at her eyes as if blowing away the tears. "Matt, too. He says that all Danny had in his life was his baseball and his dad and now he has neither," her voice broke. "I mean, he still has his dad, but it's not the same. He works all the time, and they can't bond like they used to do," she began to sniffle, and her tears fell freely.

"It's okay. It's okay," Aunt May said with a hug to Mrs. Hill. "You'll have bad days. But I promise you'll have good ones, too."

"It's just that he's like another son to me is all. I love Danny."

"I know you do," his aunt consoled. "I know."

"And Cooper," continued Matt's mom as she broke from Aunt May's hug and wiped away her tears, "I hope you'll forgive our curiosity."

Cooper had tried to step away from the women, but Mrs. Hill closed right in on him.

"We just know that somewhere inside of you there is an answer. We want to help Danny Mills find it is all. The whole town loves him," said Mrs. Hill. "He's the Wonder Kid, after all. Danny Mills, The Wonder Kid."

He tensed even as Mrs. Hill pulled him into an embrace. Not a question remained as to who the boy was. Every piece of the puzzle was nearly in place and Cooper would have to look at the mirror of his own soul in the morning when he met the real Wonder Kid.

The night was yet another restless one for Coop. He was getting tired. He needed real sleep. The dream was the usual repetitive torture and, in between the blurring out of the night vision, the memory, his own guilty conscience played at tap dancing around in his head.

Chapter 16

The Real Danny Mills

In the morning, Cooper packed his belongings and the gifts for his mom, Derek, Nicholas, and Ashley. They were just small trinkets that showed where he'd been, the kind of presents anybody brought home from travels. He shoved a handful of cotton balls into his pockets before putting the remainder of the bag into his carry-on suitcase, along with his glove. Then, after breakfast, he waited for his aunt to be ready for work.

When they arrived at the rehabilitation facility, Cooper was shocked at the appearance of the place. It was clean, but aside from that, it looked more like a psych ward out of the 1930s than a medical facility. This was nothing like the types of places he had been in when he was in the early stages of understanding his paralysis. The rooms were a grayish white with barren walls and small, singular square windows that didn't open.

"Alright, Coop," began his aunt while she pulled out a chart. "You're going to really like this boy. He's expecting you. Just talk to him. Talk to him about baseball. He'll love that. Let me take a look here. It's hard to believe it's been so long. He's been paralyzed since," she paused as she scanned the chart. "Hmmm . . . wow. How ironic. I guess I never thought about that before. He stopped moving on the same day that you began. I think I'd not mention that part to him, okay? In fact, we still don't have any answers for him. Just like you woke up moving in the middle of the night, he woke up not being able to do so."

Cooper audibly sighed with anxiety.

"It's okay, Coop. Just hang out like it's fine. You remember what it's like, right?"

Cooper nodded respectfully.

"It means an awful lot to an awful lot of people that you're here."

"Sure," said Cooper as she left him in front of the door.

He peeked into the room with the boy from his dreams. Danny's hair was combed greasily to one side. Tubes were hooked up to him and his skin was practically transparent with yellows and purples at the entrance points of all of the various tubes, needles, and other assistants. He had oxygen being fed into his nose. *Better than a ventilator*, Coop tried to reassure himself, but it didn't help. Cooper felt sorry for the once Wonder Kid. When he opened the door, a scent was in the air that made him swallow back a gag reflex unwillingly.

"It's my leg," said Danny in an off-handed tone.

Cooper didn't realize that the boy had noticed him coming in, "What?"

"The smell. It catches everyone off-guard the first time they come in. It's my leg. It's basically rotting. They're trying to heal it, but the doctors said they may have to take it soon. They do their best here, especially nurse May. But she's only here once a week. I just don't get enough movement. Sores. Infections. Again."

"May is my aunt. So, you might lose your leg?"

They say."

"Don't you have a special mattress so that you don't have pressure sores or clots or pooling?"

"They don't have that fancy stuff here!" Danny laughed. "Wouldn't be bad if I could get on the equipment more, but a lot of patients share it and it's more important to let people who could regain movement use it."

"Is that what they told you? That's not right. My aunt can—"

"Nobody told me. But the available time is what it is. And the patients are who they are. And the truth is the truth. I'm on a waiting list for some great things, though, and as for the leg, well, they have some really cool things happening with prosthetics these days, too. If I ever actually need one. Not like it would work. It would just be for my studly good looks," he smiled.

Cooper opened his mouth to say something in return, but no words seemed right.

"So, if nurse May is your aunt," Danny continued, "You must be that Cooper kid, huh?" Danny's voice became quiet and breathy, and it seemed a labor for him to talk at all, but he tried to sound upbeat.

"I must be," he said.

"Sit down," said Danny with a weak nod toward the chair by his bed. "And do you mind raising my bed a bit?"

"Um. Sure," Coop responded as he was pulled into action pressing the button that lifted Danny's head a bit to make conversation better.

Cooper couldn't believe how kind Danny Mills was. He put Coop at ease and, in no time, he noticed neither the smell, nor the whispering of the machines, nor the way his new friend couldn't move. After small talk about his aunt, the people Cooper had met in the town, and the weather, the conversation eventually turned to the subject he expected would be necessary to ease the tension, baseball.

"I had this game-winning catch last year—" Danny began.

"I know," Cooper couldn't help but say.

"You do?" asked Danny.

Tense again, "Um . . . it was national, so I read about it. My stepdad and I follow all the sports blogs," Cooper covered.

"Man, it was cool," Danny said. "It was like the whole world stopped while that flyball was falling down on me and I reached as far as I could and leapt up as high as I could, and that ball smacked against my glove so hard"

"That it stung all the way down your body to your toes until they crumpled beneath you back on the ground," finished Cooper.

"Yeah. Yeah, that's exactly it!" nodded Danny in excited agreement. "Nobody has ever described it better."

"I could imagine," said Cooper. "Do you miss it?" he asked as if he honestly wished Danny would say 'no.'

"Of course, I miss it. But I'm glad I have it to miss," said the Mills boy unexpectedly.

"What do you mean?"

"It means it happened. I gave my all and did my best. Can you imagine never being able to play ball?"

"Yes, I can," Cooper responded pointedly.

Shaking his head, "Oh. Of course. I guess you can. See, though? You're fine now. There's hope for me yet."

"To make the team again?"

"Oh, I don't care about that," Danny sputtered.

"You don't?"

Somewhat sadly, "Well, it'd be nice to be The Wonder Kid, again, sure. But mostly I just want to be ordinary, you know?"

"Yeah," Cooper agreed solemnly. "Yeah, I know exactly what you mean."

"Do you want to know what I really miss the most?" he asked.

"What?"

"Just hanging out with my dad. No championships or crowds, just having him pitch to me. Shoot! Even just having a catch. That was the best part," Danny was lost in reminiscence for a moment before snapping back into the conversation. "You said you have a stepdad, right? He throw a few with you? Or does your mom?"

Cooper thought. "No. No they haven't. I haven't," he said realizing it for the first time.

"Too bad. You're missing out," Danny said with glazed over eyes as his mind seemed to wander back to his own happy memory once again.

He was missing out? thought Cooper. How could Danny Mills lie there motionless, unable to breathe on his own, maybe about to lose his leg completely, and say that Cooper was the one who was missing out?

The personal conversation melted away once more into talk of baseball players and stats. They discussed the Arizona Diamondbacks and the Seattle Mariners and who would take the series and in how many games if the two unlikely champions were to face one another. They talked about the Washington Wonderboys and how they hadn't made it to the championship that year, but they had great talent.

The talk between the two boys lost in limbo between crippled and incredible was long and pleasant. Time ticked away to mid-morning. Cooper forgot his guilt for a moment and tried to convince himself that Danny was better at being laid up than Cooper ever was. It didn't take much to remind Coop of his selfishness, though.

"Hey, there's my son!" said a man coming into the room.

"Dad!" Danny called.

He didn't need to say it. Cooper immediately recognized the elder Mills from his dreams. He looked so much more tired now, though. His hair was grayer, and his skin was lighter, and he'd lost some weight. Mr. Mills still had the same blue eyes, although they lacked the sparkle that Cooper had noticed in them in the dream he stole.

Danny smiled up at his dad and had so much life in his face that, for an instant, Cooper could imagine him moving again. Then, almost as though Danny himself had been feeling the same thing, the smile unwillingly disappeared off of his face. He just couldn't return love to his dad the way he wanted. No matter how one tries, it's impossible to hug with a smile. Danny put that smile back in at least a feeble attempt.

"I was just stopping by," said his dad pretending not to notice that Danny's expression had fluctuated. "I had some time between jobs. But it looks like you've got company already," finished Mr. Mills while he ruffled his son's hair in the same way Cooper had witnessed in the championship dream nearly a year ago.

"Dad, this is Cooper Ridge," Danny indicated with a nod.

"Nurse May's nephew?" he said with a handshake over Danny. "We've heard all about you. You give us hope. You are the miracle," the man quickly expressed with honest eagerness. "Not that we need one, right Danny? You'll always be the Wonder Kid to me." Mr. Mills said shakily as if choking back tears.

Danny widened his smile for his dad, and it didn't look fake this time. Maybe he could learn to hug without touching. The older man simultaneously glowed with pride and grayed with heartbreak while looking down at his son on the bed. Cooper sensed an emotional moment coming on for which he did not want to be present.

"I should go," Cooper said standing up. "You'll want this chair and I have a plane to catch. It was nice meeting both of you." Then, looking at Danny, "You're going to be okay, Danny Mills," he added.

"I hope so," Daddy said with his eyes turned toward Coop.

"I know so," Cooper returned after a pause with a deep, knowing nod.

"Have a good trip," Mr. Mills offered.

Danny nodded to Cooper but the joy in his face from the moments of sharing memories had long faded away. Mr. Mills shook Cooper's hand again and Coop noticed how those roughened fingers trembled ever so slightly, while his eyes shone with clear moisture, and he nodded his close-lipped smile to Cooper.

"Well, um, bye," Cooper finished awkwardly.

He exited and peeked back through the window of the room. Almost instantaneously as the door shut behind him, Mr. Mills moved to the chair Cooper had occupied and he collapsed into it, then laid down sobbing onto his son's chest.

"Dad, don't," Danny cried with him. "Dad, it's okay. Don't make me cry. It's hard to breathe when I do," he choked out.

Cooper stared at the breathing tube attached to Danny and the tubes and wires and bags and drips going in and out of his body.

"I'm so sorry I can't afford to bring you home yet, son. I promise it will be soon. The second I've got enough to get somebody to take care of you, even if I have to work a third job. I miss having you around, son. I promise you'll come home."

"Thank you, Cooper," came Aunt May's softer-than usual voice from behind him. He quickly turned around as she asked, "Did you boys have a good conversation?"

"It was fine," Cooper answered plainly, but his mind was racing.

"Good. It means a lot to me that you visited. We really need to get you to the airport, though. Your uncle is doing a double check to make sure we've got everything in the car."

As if on cue, "Hey, I got her all loaded up down there," said Uncle Harry exiting the elevator. "You sure pack a lot for a week, Bud! You have a nice visit?"

"It was great," he replied with a stern expression.

Chapter 17

The Wakeup Call

unt May and Uncle Harry took Cooper to the airport and saw him through all the way to security where they left him with cheek kisses and tight squeezes. He waved back to them tiredly as he moved out of sight and toward his gate. It had been a trying day and he planned to sleep the whole way home to Arizona.

Somebody at the ticket counter, when he checked in, recognized him from one of the national news stories and gave him a free upgrade. He wasn't going to turn it down. More room to sleep. He requested a blanket and pillow from the flight attendant once everyone was ready for takeoff. He reached into his pocket and pulled out two cotton balls from the stash he'd stuffed into his pocket that morning. He balled up the cotton tightly and put it into his ears. Then, he blocked out the entire visit with the real Danny Mills, The Wonder Kid by shutting his heavy eyes.

He was on the bench again on that cold, Washington morning listening to the coach read off the roster. 'Matt Hill, Pitcher!" said the coach.

Next Coach read off the name of the catcher, 1st base, 2nd base, 3rd base . . .

"And for shortstop, we have a new starter this year," he began. "Danny Mills, come on over!" he called to Cooper.

The real Cooper Ridge flinched in his sleep. His ears burned and his dream blurred.

"And for shortstop, we have a new starter this year," Coach began. "Danny Mills, come on over!" he called to Cooper.

Cooper turned again and huffed away the dream's escape attempt. Clarity returned to his sleep-induced imagining.

"Danny Mills, come on over!" Coach called. The dream faded in, then out, then refocused again.

"Danny Mills, come on over!" the loop continued.

"Danny Mills. Danny Mills. Danny Mills. Danny Mills. Danny Mills. Danny Mills," the voice rang out again and again and again in his head.

There was no longer any blurriness between the replays of the dream in his mind. Coach, then Coach's face, then Coach's mouth seemed to grow larger and more and more into focus. The dream was at war, trying to bomb its way out.

"Danny Mills. Danny Mills," the nightmare name came in a nonstop stream of calls that pounded

against his throbbing ears like a hammer with each rep-
etition.

"Danny Mills, DANNY MILLS, DANNY MILLS!" the voice shouted; it grew deeper and louder and pushed so hard against his ears that Cooper felt sure his head was about to explode, pushed apart from within.

"DANNY MILLS!" the voice shrilly screamed at last.

"STOP IT!" hollered a fully awake Cooper. People all around the plane were staring.

"Sir, I don't want to have to restrain you," said a very stern flight attendant.

"I'm, I'm so sorry. I . . ." Cooper stuttered. "I was dreaming. It was . . . it was just a bad dream and my ears really hurt and . . . and I'm sorry."

The woman sized him up and looked to his ears where she spotted the cotton balls, "Oh. Cotton. A lot of people experience ear pain on planes. But if you dis-turb the passengers again, I will have to get the air mar-shal involved. Is that understood."

"Yes, ma'am," he nodded. "I understand."

Cooper relaxed as best he could as he pulled the cotton from his ears and sat up. He wouldn't be sleeping on this trip after all.

"Wait," he called after the flight attendant. "When we land, will it still be daylight?"

"For a bit."

"Good," he said. "I have something I have to do."

Cooper stared out the window for the rest of the flight. Unwilling tears filled the bottoms of his eyes, but he stubbornly blinked them away as he inhaled and exhaled, feeling each breath as it filled and then left his body. His plane landed while the sun still shone in the Arizona sky. *No sky in the world compared to the desert before sunset*, he thought.

Derek and his mom greeted him on the other side of security with hugs.

"We missed you so much," April gushed. "I hated how we left things. I'm so sorry."

Cooper held back tears of emotional and physical exhaustion, "No, Mom, you were right. I'm the one who is sorry. I'm sorry. And to you, too, Derek. I'm so sorry."

"It's okay, Coop," Derek said before asking, "Did you sleep on the plane?"

"Couldn't," replied Cooper truthfully.

Honesty felt good.

"I can never sleep on planes," his stepdad said as he took Cooper's bag, and they made their ways to the baggage claim. "My ears pop like crazy."

"Tell me about it," said Cooper.

After collecting his bag, the three drove home to detailed discussion around Cooper's trip. He talked about Aunt May and Uncle Harry and their new place. He told them about the sights he saw. And, of course, he shared stories about his last day in Washington.

"Derek, these guys were amazing," Cooper gushed. "You wouldn't believe they're a little league team the way they play," he said.

Cooper would have gladly talked more about the Wonderboys, but the distraction didn't last.

"May told me you talked to that poor boy, Danny Miller, too," April said.

"Mills," Cooper corrected.

"Nice guy?" Derek asked.

After a thoughtful pause, "The best," said Cooper.

His mom cautiously asked, "How's he doing?"

"He, uh . . ." Cooper stopped, not knowing what to say.

"Not so good, huh?" Derek presumed.

With a reach back to touch her son in consolation, April added, "That must have been hard, Bud',"

"Yeah. It was," Cooper said honestly again; this honesty thing might even catch back on. "It's just that everybody thinks I might have the answer," he shared.

"That's a lot of pressure," said Derek.

"It is," Cooper said, "But maybe I really can help.

"Sure you can, son," April said affectionately. "You already made such a difference by visiting that community and bringing them hope."

"I need to do more," Cooper said.

"You just do what you think is best," said Derek.

"Yeah," Cooper sighed heavily. "What I think is best," Cooper finished, mostly to himself.

The rest of the trip home remained quiet as Cooper looked out the window and his mind drifted to his evening plans.

Chapter 18

Having A Catch

When they got home, Cooper took his things to his room and he began to unpack. His bedroom was a little cluttered. He'd have to take care of that. He set out his gifts for his mom and stepdad. He got his mom a snowglobe because his aunt said it would remind her of their childhoods in Wisconsin. Derek got a signed book from one of the local bookstores that Uncle Harry had taken Cooper to on the visit. He had a single Pacific Ocean seashell for Ashley. At the time he'd picked it out, he had romantic imaginings of offering to take her to the ocean one day. He laid each of the gifts he had out on his dresser neatly so that they could be easily accessed and pointed out.

The ball from the Championship game would be for Nicholas, but there was something else Cooper had to do with it first. He pulled his glove out from his carry-on suitcase and put it on, pounding the already well-worn leather with his fist. It was still slightly dusty from the Washington field, and he was surprised how the scent had come home with him and made him feel like he was still there.

He took out the baseball from the Wonderboys coach and he dropped it into his glove a couple of times. He loved the sound of the ball as it echoed hollowly in the glove. Then, he headed to the kitchen.

"Hey Mom? Derek?" he asked casually. "You guys want to have a catch?" he asked.

"Yes!" they said nearly in unison.

"We'd love to," April said, barely able to contain herself. Derek had already left the room and was returning with gloves for he and April, as well as a ball.

"I have a ball, Derek," Coop said.

"Whatever you want," Derek said, putting his ball onto the counter and following Cooper out with April.

The end-of-summer air was calm, and the world seemed to stand still, keeping the sun hanging like a giant fiery ornament in the sky for even longer than it should have remained there. It was almost as though the day stretched on for just Cooper and his family while they shared the seasonal pastime at the end of the summer season.

He, his mom, and Derek laughed and talked and tossed the ball between one another. Derek worked Cooper at fielding the ball high, low, and to each side. Cooper whipped the stitched sphere to his mom with all of his might and she acted as though the catch stung.

When they finally went in, only after the sun had long gone, the dusk had faded, and the fluorescent streetlights began to blink on, it was with sore shoulders and dry throats that needed quenching with sweet tea. The three enjoyed burgers done on the grill topped with lettuce and tomato. Cooper ate slowly, savoring every bite. Dinner conversation was buzzing with the reliving of tales from the summer. It was the perfect end to the perfect day in a perfect dream.

Later that night, Cooper sat on the edge of his bed holding his baseball glove. It had been his constant companion for months. He felt the soft leather by running his fingers over each curve of the digits. He closed his eyes and took in every worn spot, every stitch, every smooth surface, and every inch that had gone bald straight down to the linen-like stubble left behind when the oiled, tanned surface had served its time. He had given his best with the glove. Having finally had a catch with Derek and his mom, it had given him something in return.

At the touch of his glove, Cooper mourned. He mourned the loss of the person he once was. Without the use of most of his body, he never had a problem sharing his heart. He had been grateful for the things that he did have. He didn't rush. He took time for people and activities that mattered. With his arms and legs, though, he had grown selfish and allowed others to suffer for his gifts. His mom and Derek who just wanted to enjoy a life of movement with him? All he could do was think of being away from them, being away from the home that had protected him for so long. He wanted to run, to keep his new life to himself.

Cooper also mourned the possibility that the dreams would never return again; the dreams that gave him the gift of movement and so many other joyful moments.

Last, he mourned the person he could have been if he'd remembered to use that most important part of himself when he'd gained the use of every part. His heart. *No more,* he thought. *I know what matters now. I know what's best. I just hope it's not too late.*

Cooper rose from his bed with the glove, and he walked over to his top dresser drawer. He put his glove in the drawer and then closed it. Coop took the bag of cotton balls out of his carry-on and brought it to the bathroom.

When he returned to his room, he picked up all of his things from the floor and straightened everything to make a clear path and neatly kept area. In his closet, his chair was folded up with his bat boy uniform from Nicholas's team lying across the top of it. Cooper hung up the uniform, trying not to focus on the wheelchair, and then he took from his closet the signed bat and his old, loose yo-yo. Next, he turned off the closet's light and shut its door.

He went to the bathroom one more time, working to fully clear his bladder and bowels, just in case. He even stopped at the closet full of disability supplies and made sure that the most important things were accessible. His mom had held onto these things that he'd wished to discard. Doctors had told her to give his new movement a full year before donating the supplies and equipment. He hated that there was always a thought at the back of her mind that he could end up back in the chair. Tonight, though, he was grateful that these things were still in their little medical gift shop.

There's just one thing left to do, thought Cooper as he looked at his bedroom window. Determined to follow through, he crossed the room. He balanced the bat against his window ledge and put his yo-yo upon the nightstand beneath his lamp. Cooper turned the lock on the window and opened it, not just an inch or two, but as wide as it would go. A gust of fresh Arizona air rushed the room and convicted him in his decision. The tassel like ends of the pennants on his wall fluttered lightly.

Cooper propped up his pillows and changed into a newly cleaned pair of pajamas. He told his smart speaker not to go off in the morning. He had no desire to wake to face the next day. He turned on his pressure changing mattress that had been silenced months ago. The sound of the tiny motor and whispering of air flow began immediately. It was a resigned sound. When his mom and Derek came in to say goodnight, Cooper pulled his mom tightly to him in a bear hug and he squeezed with all his might.

"My goodness," she laughed. "What is this all about?"

"Nothing," he said while still holding onto her. "Just wanted to give you a really good hug."

"Is your mattress on?" asked Derek.

"That plane ride was so rough, I thought it might help," he said, and it wasn't technically a lie.

"Alright Coop," Derek said just as the teen finally released his mom. "You sleep well," he said with a squeeze to Cooper's arm that his stepson allowed to penetrate his senses and swim in his veins before also pulling Derek into a hug, as well.

As the two left, Cooper couldn't look at them. He held his eyes shut as if already sleeping. It would take some time before any actual sleep arrived. He tossed and turned, fighting the shuteye that would end in stillness. He blinked awake and sat up to look at his watch. It was 12:28 A.M. *Time of death,* he thought.

Cooper laid back down to face his window, breathing in the outdoor evening air and indulging the feeling of it in his chest. Eventually, tears and exhaustion made heavy first his eyes and then the rest of his body, and Cooper nodded into the damning slumber.

Chapter 19

Catching The Tear

It seemed that only minutes had passed in the dreamless sleep of night. At least he thought it was dreamless. He couldn't recall the Wonderboys' field or Matt Hill, or Coach, or the try-outs, or the name. Although he was sure that they had just shut, Cooper's eyes snapped open quickly to the sounds of his mother's ringtone down the hall. In addition to the ringing, Cooper felt a warm tickle in the ear that was not against his pillow.

He didn't move.

He lay numb and still while staring at the window. He saw in the soft orange light of early dawn a very dim, weak firefly making a slow and tipsy flight out of his bedroom window. Cooper's throat grew a suffocating lump. His mouth tasted salty, and he felt hot moisture welling up in his blurry, burning eyes. He pursed his lips tightly and swallowed hard while the phone continued to ring on.

"Hello?" his mom answered at last.

"It's your sis', April!" came the voice.

Cooper wished she wasn't on speaker. He didn't want to hear the call. He was sure what it might be.

"I meant to text you last night, May," his mom said. "Cooper got in just fine. Sorry."

"It's okay. It's great news. Just happened. You'll never believe it! I've just told Harry and I still find it difficult to imagine it happening twice. Twice!" she said exhilarated. "I just had to say it out loud again."

Cooper listened stoically to the conversation. Listening would be something he would have to get used to again. He steadied his breathing.

"What?" asked Derek who must have just joined his wife.

"It's amazing!"

"What is it already, May?" April prompted.

"It's that boy Danny Mills. The boy that Cooper just visited." Aunt May exclaimed.

"Yes?" asked Derek.

"He woke up this morning and—" his aunt broke off, choking back emotion.

"Are you okay?" April asked in concern. "Is the boy okay?

"I'm great. I'm great and, you won't believe this but—"

Cooper knew what she would say before the words finished coming out of her mouth.

"—so is Danny," she finished emotionally. "He's great, too. He can walk, April. Danny Mills can walk. He woke up the same way our Cooper did. His dad just called me and he's going to be fine. And he was not in a good place, April. He had serious issues as a result of his paralysis, but they're all just . . . gone."

Cooper tried to block out the rest of the conversation. His head ached deeply. He blinked his eyes shut while his lips began to tremble and the tears that had formed in the bottom of his eyes began seeping out of his closed lids, streaming down to be absorbed by his pillow. The crawling wetness tickled as tears from his other eye toward the ceiling made their way over the bridge of his nose while he lay on his side. The tear ran across his face and down the length of the cheekbone on the other side of his face. As the itch grew in intensity, instinctively, in that moment, Cooper reached up and wiped it away. He gasped at the sight of his own hand in front of his face.

"I . . ." he said to himself.

Cooper sat bolt upright in his bed disbelievingly. He sniffled and brushed away the remaining tears on his face. Then he stood.

Immediately, Cooper's legs fell out from under him like snapped toothpicks. He clunked loudly and heavily to the floor.

"Coop?" April called. "Hey, May, I gotta go. We'll talk later. Congratulations. I'm so happy for everyone. Please pass on our best," she rushed the words out.

"Will do! B'bye!" Aunt May happily finished before Cooper heard April and Derek in the hallway.

"Cooper are you okay?" asked Derek.

"Why are you on the floor?" April wondered.

"I don't know," said Cooper truthfully. "I fell. My legs don't feel right."

Chapter 20

Cooper Ridge, Ordinary Kid

Two weeks and many tests later, Cooper, his mom, and Derek sat opposite the same doctor who was befuddled months ago with the miracle of Cooper Ridge, The Wonder Kid. They awaited results and ideas and answers.

"I don't know what to tell you," the doctor said. "AGAIN!" he joked. "I swear I really do know what I'm doing, but you are unique, young man," he said to Cooper. Then, to his folks, "There is nothing wrong with your son. In fact, it's quite the contrary. When you came to me in March, every test I performed seemed to tell me that your son shouldn't be moving at all. His nerves simply weren't carrying information the way that they should. Yet then, he was like an athlete. Now, he's . . . well . . . he's limited again. Disabled, though certainly not the way he had been. The difference now is that his nerves *are* working."

"How did that change?" April asked.

"Perhaps they've repaired themselves because of all of their use. He's been an active boy and the human body is amazing. It's been known to heal itself with strong physical therapy and this summer has certainly served as that for him. All I know is that this at least makes some sense. That," shrugged the doctor with the same stumped expression he had in March, "and it's the only theory I've got at this point."

"What does this mean? Will he ever be like he was, again?" asked Derek.

"Oh, I see no reason he'd become paralyzed again," answered the doctor.

"No," Derek shook his head and looked to Cooper. "I mean . . . um . . . I don't want to sound ungrateful, but—"

"You mean will he be like he was in summer," nodded the doctor in understanding. "Anything is possible. If anyone has proven that, it's you, Cooper," he smiled to the teen. "His legs work, Mr. and Mrs. Lowell. They're just weak. He'll need the walker until he's strong again and, honestly, I can't tell you how long that is. Months or maybe even years. I'd have him practice walking without it for a little bit each day and I'd continue the same sort of therapy you provided when he was in his chair. I'm sorry I don't have more answers for you. Do you have more questions for me?" he asked.

"I just wish I understood why," April sighed with a reassuring squeeze around her son's shoulders.

"To that, I'll only repeat what I said in March. Medicine doesn't always have the answers and if I were in your shoes, I'd simply be grateful for every moment I had."

"I definitely am," Cooper smiled.

April and Derek turned to him and smiled, as well. They were in this together as a family.

The three left very slowly as each step was one of learning for Cooper. He willed every muscle to move one leg forward at time in an almost dragging motion. Cooper grimaced through the concentrated struggle, but never once complained about it.

Each day, Cooper worked hard at becoming stronger. He earned every inch he moved forward, whether it was cheering in front of the stands at Nicholas's games, taking a neighborhood walk at night, or even moving across his own bedroom to turn on his light switch.

His overhead light and his bedside lamp were the only lights in his room, now – no longer were there fireflies. The dreams never came again after that summer, at least not the magical ones made up of special memories. Cooper didn't mind. For, each morning, he put his own arms around his mom. Each day, he used his own hand to shake that of his stepdad. Each afternoon, he'd slap his best friend on the back or shoulder chummily when they played video games together.

And, on his own two feet, he walked down the street. He practiced adding a few extra steps each day without his walker.

One night, Ashley even joined him.

"Mind if I walk with you?" the beautiful girl asked.

"Really? Now? I'm pretty slow these days," Cooper said.

"I don't mind. I always liked how I could slow down with you. How we could just talk and not be a part of the rest of my crazy rushed life. You heard all those stories about school."

"I always thought you wanted that life," Cooper said.

"I don't dislike that life, Coop," Ashley smiled. "I just also liked what you and I share. And I only shared it with you. I've really missed you these last few months. You were doing a lot of new things, but I never needed something different than what we already were. So, like I asked, do you mind if I walk with you?"

Cooper nodded, "I'd like that.

Ashley walked beside him, talking about her day and week while Cooper concentrated on each inch. He knew he'd make it to the end of the block one day and he knew it was a destination that was earned and not stolen. While he worked, just as they had when he was paralyzed and how they had when he was an athlete – those in his life loved him. Now, perhaps with a better understanding than ever before thanks to a conversation with the real Danny Mills, he loved them unconditionally and selflessly in return.

On his evening walks, Cooper often saw the fireflies flickering in the distance, blinking beside the open windows of children and others in the neighborhood. His mouth would turn up sweetly as he was overcome with quiet contentment for the secret of a fantasy world that he would always keep.

He was no longer Cooper Ridge, The Wonder Kid and he never would be. He was, however, Cooper Ridge, Ordinary Kid.

A flood of warm satisfaction rushed through him when Cooper realized that he was at peace with this title . . . perhaps even at joy. As this thought of true happiness came over him, he saw a single firefly, far brighter and larger than any he had seen before, appear seemingly out of nowhere in front of him. It floated dreamily away from him and rose in a gentle drift up to the starry sky above.

The End

About The Author

Known to friends and colleagues as **"RED,"** the author of more than 60 still available genre fiction and general audience works has written for nearly three decades in playwriting, children's books, sportswriting, biography, leadership, ministry, writing resources, fiction, and more.

Red is a member of the *International Association of Science Fiction and Fantasy Authors (IASFA)*, *Women's Fiction Writers Association (WFWA)*, *20Booksto50K*, *National Association of Independent Writers and Editors (NAIWE)*, and other respected author organizations. See her website to catch her on tour or book her for a visit.

Red has been many-times award-nominated, including a Newberry Medal, and she is a 13-time #1 Bestselling author of 100+ titles, through traditional and independent publishers, across many genres, with combined sales of over 600,000 books.

Before young adult and adult genre fiction as JERI SHEPHERD, she wrote (and continues to write) as REJI LABERJE as a solo author and co-author alongside celebrities, athletes, and leaders of industry. As her friend, one-time co-author, and five-time publishing colleague ESPN's Dick "Dickie V" Vitale says of her:

"She is a dedicated, talented, and organized writer you would be proud to be associated with. I highly recommend her in every way. She is multi-talented, and her work is very creative."

Author Photo By: Arpit Mehta

Red is a veteran, wife, mother, and grandmother with interests ranging from nerdy to outdoorsy to artsy to trendy,

Learn more at: **www.jerishepherdbooks.com**
And follow the author on social media:
https://linktr.ee/FaultLinesBooks

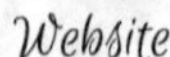

Website   *Social Media*

www.ingramcontent.com/pod-product-compliance
Lightning Source LLC
Chambersburg PA
CBHW072112300726

48975CB00003B/781